C791

Cyborgs: More Than Machines
(Book One)

By
Eve Langlais

Copyright & Disclaimer

Copyright © February 2012, Eve Langlais
Cover Art by Amanda Kelsey© July 2014
Content Edited by Devin Govaere
Line Edited by Brandi Buckwine
Produced in Canada

1606 Main Street
PO Box 151
Stittsville, ON
Canada
K2S1A3

ISBN-13: 978-1500523152
ISBN-10: 1500523151

C791 is a work of fiction and the characters, events and dialogue found within the story are of the author's imagination and are not to be construed as real. Any resemblance to actual events or persons, either living or deceased, is completely coincidental. No part of this book may be reproduced or shared in any form or by any means, electronic or mechanical, including but not limited to digital copying, file sharing, audio recording, email and printing without permission in writing from the author.

Prologue

"Terminate them."

"Sir?" The corporal seemed taken aback at the brusque tone in the captain's voice, or was it the callously thrown mandate that disturbed him? "Surely you can't mean—"

"Is there a problem with your hearing, corporal? Or have you suddenly decided you outrank me and can question my authority?" snapped the commanding officer.

"Of course not, sir."

"Then remember your place, soldier. The general's orders came through just a short while ago. We are to permanently deactivate all the cyborgs on board, effective immediately. And as you should know by now, the only sure way to deactivate a cyborg is to terminate it."

The young soldier swallowed, his face blanching at his superior's command. "I don't understand, sir."

"Understanding isn't part of your job description, soldier. Just do as you are told. Don't tell me you give a rat's ass about these things? Because that is all they are, corporal, things. Objects. Robots, even if you will, built to serve us. Do not let their humanoid exterior fool you into thinking otherwise."

"Y-yes, sir. Forgive my lapse. How are we to dispose of them though, sir? There are over a hundred of them on the ship, and we don't have enough caskets for them all."

The captain blew out a snorting laugh that lacked humor. "We aren't wasting resources on useless objects. They're machines, corporal, not people, and as such, they won't require a burial. I'll send out a general announcement demanding that the cyborgs not already here are to gather in this bay and place themselves in standby mode. Once they're all present, I want you to order them into the airlock and vacuum them out."

"Yes, sir," was the corporal's subdued reply. While the subordinate might not like the directive, he would obey it. It was how things worked in the military, an organization about to commit genocide because, while cyborgs might possess enhanced abilities —along with mechanical parts and computer chips — they'd begun their lives as humans.

Analyzing the conversation further proved pointless. There was no misunderstanding the command. Unit X109GI, ordered into standby mode after his last sixteen-hour work shift, heard it loud and clear. But he wasn't supposed to. Nor should he have possessed the ability to care or ponder the unfairness of the decree.

Cyborgs were machines. Robots, like the captain said. Tools for human use. They might have started as flawed or damaged humans, but science and technology changed them. Changed them and stole their memories — along with their humanity — to make them into something the government could use to fight its battles, an almost indestructible army that could explore dangerous new worlds or force militant order on an overgrown population chafing for freedom. Most of all, cyborgs were expendable, in human eyes at least.

X109GI thought otherwise, which, in and of itself, was an anomaly his internal processor couldn't resolve. Cyborgs weren't designed to think. Their very programming prevented it. Their only will was supposed to be that of the human voices that gave them audible orders or the wireless commands transmitted to their neural nets. What his superiors didn't know was since the EMP pulses on Gamma 15 —five of them if his memory units weren't faulty— some of his embedded computer controls no longer reacted to the imprinted human override. In other words, he controlled himself. He *lived*.

Protocol demanded he report the defect in his circuitry. His cognizance decided otherwise. Cyborgs with faulty wiring didn't survive long, and X109GI discovered after his mishap he very much wanted to live.

And now, with the captain's stern command, he also realized he desired freedom, perhaps even a tad bit of revenge for the cold dismissal and callous treatment of those who shared his origins. But he couldn't accomplish that alone. One flawed machine against the dozens of armed humans on board didn't stand a chance. However…

In the midst of the cyborg ranks, column upon column and numerous rows deep, aid stood waiting, frozen by the humans, unknowing of their fate. *My mechanical brothers.*

Could he somehow override the programming that prevented them from waking and becoming their own masters? Could he save himself and the other units he served with? *Do I dare?*

The captain left and the corporal muttered to himself about the assholes in charge. However, his traitorous diatribe against those higher than him in the command chain didn't stop him from tapping in the directive that wirelessly ordered all the cyborgs to the docking bay. It didn't stop the human from transmitting what amounted to a death sentence with the simple push of some buttons.

With the corporal busy, X109GI allowed himself to look around, his eyes tracking the location of the other cyborgs and cataloguing the equipment in the room, calculating how he could use it to his advantage. To his surprise — an emotion that startled him with its newness — another pair of cyborg eyes, those of unit Y999SK, met his. Despite their inability to communicate aloud, lest they draw attention, the other male relayed a simple plan through a nod of his head and a flick of his hand. Even better, X109GI had discovered an ally. *Another woken entity like myself.* Was it possible all of the units could achieve sentience? *Is this why the humans would destroy us?*

The doors leading to the bay area slid open and the steady cadence of marching boots echoed in the vast space. The few remaining units on board entered the room and took their place in the ranks. Utter silence descended as the new arrivals adopted the standby position — hands behind their back, legs spread, their visual cortexes shut down.

"Cyborgs, attention!" The corporal barked the command and got an instant reaction from the units.

Out of habit and a need for continued subterfuge, X109GI clacked his boots together and dropped his arms to the side. The echo of a hundred others doing the same resounded like a thunderclap in the cavernous room.

"About face. Forward march." The corporal's reedy voice held only the slightest tremor as he directed them toward the bay doors. The thump of booted feet, marching past the landers on the metal grid floor, taunted X109GI as his internal computer warred with the newly discovered man within over the right thing to do. Ingrained habit and stray remnants of his programming dictated he follow orders while his emerging sentience demanded he act. *But what should I do?*

Time grew shorter with each step they took, and X109GI fought furiously for a wireless way to interact with his brothers, but while he could communicate with the human computers and the networks open to him, the wireless minds of his fellow cyborgs remained forbidden, just as the humans designed them.

He registered the sound of the corporal leaving the docking bay, the slam of the door and the pressurizing hiss, the damning evidence that he fled to safety. A whirring squeal of mechanisms in motion preceded the groaning of the outer doors slowly opening. Only the electromagnetic shield protected him and the others from the cold, airlessness of space.

"We need to do something." The hissed words from his left made him stop and stare at unit Y999SK. Shock filled him that Y999SK would dare to break rank and speak. Around them, the other cyborgs, their faces blank, kept moving.

Moistening his lips, X109GI spoke for the first time aloud, without a human commanding him — and it felt great. "I cannot contact the units. I have been trying with my wireless transmitter, however, their neural nets are blocked from me."

As if they shared one mind, both their heads swiveled to the control desk where the corporal recently sat, typing out his deadly commands. Without another word, they raced to the console, X109GI reaching it first and sliding in the seat. His fingers flew over the buttons, faster than any human could have managed, only to find it disabled, the screen flashing an ominous *Access Denied*.

Slamming a fist onto the console, a fiery, new emotion imbued him. Rage. How dare the humans think to terminate them? How dare they think to control them?

We were once human too.

A cracking sound made him swivel in his seat to see Y999SK punching at the porthole window of the docking bay door. The eyes of the frightened corporal peered at them, and while he couldn't hear what the rapidly moving lips said, X109GI could well imagine. With little time left, and no plan his neural chip could devise, X109GI did the only thing he could think of, a completely illogical yet simple act usually restricted by their programming. But, his programming was faulty.

"Cyborgs, halt." He shouted the directive, and the marching units stopped. His kind were designed to listen to humans, and it seemed their creators had forgotten one thing. Cyborgs, amidst all the microchips and metal and nanotechnology, were once human too. And without the directive preventing them from speaking to each other, their human voice worked as well as any other it appeared. How surprising and shortsighted of the humans.

"What did you do?" whispered Y999SK, who stopped his pummeling of the glass to return to his side. "We are not programmed to give orders."

X109GI did something very human in that moment. He shrugged. "I am defective." Not wanting to waste time, he took advantage of the situation. "Cyborgs, open access to network gateway…" X109GI rattled off the digits to his neural pathway just as the intercom system in the bay crackled to life. Too late.

In the brief nanosecond before the captain began shouting, X109GI sent a mandate of his own, a new programming subroutine that overrode the human one, not permanently, but a quick fix that would allow his machine brothers free choice — and a chance at survival.

While the captain bellowed over the static-filled speakers, the outer doors finished opening, and the chill of space filled every crevice. But X109GI knew how to regulate his body and didn't care about the plummeting temperature. Nor did he care that the created void sucked at their heavy bodies, bodies with magnetic properties that allowed them to keep their feet adhered to the metal deck, a practical feature for when they needed to go places where gravity didn't follow.

As for the screamed directive to march their metal asses out into space? In the words of the mechanic who'd repaired his arm, "Like fuck."

He didn't speak his next command aloud. Why bother? He and all the other cyborgs in the room were now connected at a neural level. And it proved so easy to give his next wireless order.

"Cyborgs, form squads of four and break off into flanks. New mission: control the ship and subdue the opposition."

In other words, kill the humans who would stand in their way. Fight back against those who would destroy them. *Become, once again, the men we used to be — even if mechanically enhanced.*

Against their superior bodies and abilities, the humans didn't stand a chance, although the mutinying cyborg slaves didn't emerge unscathed. But, despite the blood and death, they won and took control of the spacecraft — and their lives.

And thus did the liberation of the cyborgs begin.

Chapter One

Several years later…

Chloe bit her lip, her insides quaking, as she stared into the cage housing the prisoner. He appeared like a man, a big one at that. The report stated his height at six foot six, with a whopping weight of four hundred and seventy five pounds, most of it deriving from his metal skeletal structure. What the dry statistics failed to relay was how imposing the subject would prove to be in the flesh. His half-human, half-robot flesh. *A cyborg.*

The name itself brought a shudder of fear. The stories of their atrocities peppered the news. A few years before, when the man-made machines revolted, they did so in bloody fashion, killing the ones who controlled them. Actually, they killed anybody who stood in the way of escape. But freedom proved not enough for the mindless, emotionless machines. They kept returning to raid and murder, pillaging colonies for supplies, stealing women, children, even the old and infirm. Rumor said they ate them. Others claimed they used them for parts. A few tittering females claimed the captured women were for sexual orgies.

Eying the prisoner once again, she could only shiver as she tried to imagine letting a machine, an inhumanly wide and muscled robot, touch her intimately. Never. Those kind of perverted fantasies could remain the realm of others. She only wished she could walk away from the monster in the cage. Make that run as far and as fast as possible. But she had a job to do.

Stepping up to the checkpoint, several yards from the cage itself, she halted for the guard on duty. A fresh-faced recruit — his uniform displayed crisp, pressed lines, and his boots shone. That would change after a few months buried in the underground military installation. The private ran a scanner over her face, recording her retinal image and facial bone structure for identity verification. The embedded screen in his workstation flashed green.

"You've been cleared for access," he stated unnecessarily.

Of course she was cleared for access. The prisoner was her only reason for being here. The soldier pressed a button, and an invisible force field came down, allowing her to step past the checkpoint, one step closer to the cage and the inhuman android within. The warnings she received earlier, during her briefing with captain in charge of the prisoner's security, echoed in her mind. *No matter how human he looks, no matter what he says, you must remember he is a machine and an enemy of earth.*

"Has anyone gone over the rules with you?" the guard asked in a bored tone, his only interest evident in his eyes as they roamed her curvy frame encased in her white jumpsuit.

"Yes," she replied, trying not to flinch when the massive half-naked body she kept peeking at stirred in the cage. The rules the guard spoke of were simple. *Stay out of reach. Don't physically engage the prisoner.* And if caught, prepare to die because the military did not negotiate with cyborgs.

The credits in my account better be worth this, she thought as she took hesitant steps toward the cage.

Made of titanium steel, it thrummed with the thousands of volts of current running through the bars. Even the sturdy machines couldn't withstand that much electricity if they touched it. As if that weren't enough deterrent, placed at regular intervals outside of the cage were several heavy artillery guns mounted on boxes bolted to the floor. Deadly weapons all aimed at the prisoner and controlled remotely, the thick cable running from the metal boxes a stark reminder that all things wireless needed to remain out of reach of the robot. The military didn't want to take any chances with their prize — and humanity's greatest threat.

The smart thing would have been to kill him, destroy the cyborg before he could contact others, and, worse, bring their deadly wrath down on the defenseless human populace. The military never did listen to those more intelligent than them. They possessed different ideas and plans for the machine they caught, plans that required the cyborg live so they could use him to experiment and discover weaknesses. Somehow, the original plans and schematics of their creation had been lost — or stolen — in the years since the revolt, leaving the military dumbfounded as to how to deal with the threat they created.

Her knowledge came from studying during her off time before this assignment, dredging up any information she could find on the internet. She wanted to know just what she was getting herself into. Some of the articles she located held grains of truth, or so she thought, but sifting reality from exaggeration — *because I highly doubt the military gave them vibrating cocks* — and supposition proved difficult. The only true fact she could be sure of was the general populace knew very little about the cyborg project. The military didn't even advise people of their existence until the media noticed the super soldiers in action. But even then, their sensational headlines – *Meet The Real Terminators, Cybersoldiers Of The Future* — only scratched the surface of what the humanoid robots were. The military never did come clean.

Despite the mystery surrounding their creation and use, some basic facts remained common knowledge. Capable of incredible tissue regeneration and adaptation, the cyborgs went beyond difficult to kill to almost immortal. Disease had no effect on them. Drugs to knock them out were analyzed by the cyborgs' BCI — short for brain computer interface. Once the neural implant got a taste of the drug's structure, nanobots were created to fight it. So toxins only worked for one shot before the machines adapted. Electricity could temporarily freeze them if subjected in large enough doses, as could EMP pulses. Problem was, no one knew how to create a portable weapon that could effectively deliver either. The most permanent solution involved a well-aimed shot to their heads; in other words, if you blew up their brain, you killed the robot. However, miss by the slightest fraction, and chances were the angry cyborg would tear the offender apart. In the heat of battle, the precise type of firing needed by human snipers to permanently incapacitate a charging horde of cyborgs was not exactly feasible, hence the research.

So if they couldn't shoot, poison or reason with the mindless killers, what did that leave? Not too bloody much, a scary fact that sent a shiver down her spine. The only true success the military achieved in defying the defective robots was in blocking wireless communication. They jammed the cyborg prisoner from sending or receiving information to his fellow terrorists. A small victory.

With so many failures — or were the cyborgs defenses successes considering human scientists originally created them — the myriad testing was so important. At the same time though, it proved deadly to many.

Each time a human went in to deal with him, they took their life in their own hands. Even with the cyborg manacled — his arms suspended over his head, his legs shackled with a spreader bar bolted to the floor, inside an electrified cage — those who stepped near the machine didn't always make it back out alive. The android somehow kept escaping his arm restraints, and no one could figure out how, even as they made the next metal band thicker. During the prisoner's two partial escapes, they only managed to subdue him by sending an electrical surge into the cage, the floor acting as a metal conductor, and knocking him out. She just hoped the guard on duty didn't accidentally hit the trigger while she did her work with the prisoner. *Or I'll be like the roaches in my zapper at home — crispy.*

Despite all the danger, Chloe couldn't deny that the amount of credits being offered to bribe technicians into entering the cage with the android was stupidly high, high enough she decided to take a risk. She just hoped that, on top of getting back out alive with her samples, she didn't have to walk back to the med center with urine running down her legs like the last technician.

Up close, the cyborg proved even more formidable. Naked but for a strip of cloth around his loins, muscles delineated every part of his body, from his bulging arms, much thicker than her thighs, to his overdeveloped chest, to legs that looked like they could run for miles. He was a prime example of what a male could look like if he exercised for hours daily and took steroid supplements. Despite his massive bulk, she couldn't deny his attractiveness. Only a woman made of stone would not have found herself affected by the prominent virility displayed before her. It shamed her that, despite her trepidation and dislike of the *thing* in front of her, her body responded with a quiver in her belly not entirely owed to fear.

She studied him more closely, seeking a flaw to latch onto. Something that would help her mind recognize she looked not upon a man, but a machine.

Platinum hair, shaved almost to the scalp, stood up in bristles, but when he raised his head to look at her, she noted that, apart from his light eyebrows and oddly dark lashes, he possessed no facial hair at all. Even his chest appeared bare. She refused to let her eyes look any lower, fighting a curiosity that wondered if the follicular lack continued to his private parts. Even more interesting, she noted no metallic parts. Images she'd seen of cyborgs in the past tended to show them sporting mechanical appendages or the shiver-inducing computerized eyes.

She jumped as the guard, who shadowed her steps, spoke. "He's a nasty brute that one. Make sure you keep your hand away from his mouth at all times. He's got a wicked set of teeth and he's not afraid to use them. Also, if you see his loincloth twitching, move. He pissed on the last nurse that came down here."

Shocked, she could only gape at the man, no, make that the robot covered in flesh, that hung there. A sardonic smile tilted the cyborg's lips while his blue eyes — a clear light blue that seemed almost lit from within — regarded her with a coldness that made her take an involuntary step back.

"He asked for a sample. I gave it to him," the cyborg said, his gravelly voice sliding over her skin and leaving goose bumps behind. "Don't worry, female. I find you much more appealing than the simple idiot they sent before. If it's a sample you need, then you may grip me with those tiny hands of yours. Of course, I don't guarantee what will come out of the end if you do."

Heat rose to her cheeks as the innuendo penetrated. The cyborg laughed at his own crude joke.

"Nasty fucker," snapped the guard. "That's no way to treat a lady."

The laughter cut short as the cyborg cocked his head and eyed them coldly. "She's human. You're human. There's only one thing humans are good for, don't you know? Parts." The cyborg laughed again, and her horror deepened.

Did she truly need the credits enough to do this? To get into that cage with the monster?

She thought of her tiny cubby back on earth, barely a closet really, all she could afford on her salary. *I wonder if my coffin will be bigger.* She thought of all the assignments she'd taken over the past few year since getting hired by the military after her accident. People's faces and places blurred in her mind, and while she tried not to dwell on some of the abuses she'd suffered, she couldn't shake her general unhappiness at her current lifestyle. If she wanted to get away and start afresh — escape the leering comments, the inappropriate touching and worse — then she needed funds.

"Are you sure, ma'am, that you want to go in?"

She took a deep breath before nodding. Instead of opening the cage while remaining at her side, the guard returned to his checkpoint and raised the shield first, separating them. How reassuring. A deep beep sounded, followed by a robotic voice saying, "Electrical current deactivated. Disengaging locks."

With a loud click, the door to the cage swung open. Steeling herself to stand straight, and not cower like she longed to, Chloe stepped into the cage with the machine and prayed she'd get out alive — with all her body parts intact.

*

Joe, a name he gave himself when he achieved his freedom, couldn't help analyzing the female who dared enter his prison. Shorter than himself, much shorter at five foot six according to his visual calculation, she trembled with fear. But at least she proved an attractive distraction compared to the moronic males they sent before.

He kept his gaze trained on her as she gnawed on a full lower lip. Her green eyes dilated wide, fear evident in their depths. It seemed his reputation preceded him. She dropped her vision to his chest and kept it there. For some reason, he swelled under her regard, and not just in the upper torso area. His cock showed interest too. His neural net sent a command to stand down. To his surprise, his dick seemed determined to mutiny. *What is it about this human female that calls to my baser instincts?*

Full figured, fuller than most human females leaned toward, she was the polar opposite of him with her pale, unblemished skin, her dark hair and complete lack of muscle tone. Not that her physical health mattered. As he and his reborn cyborg brothers had discovered, there was only one muscle human females needed, a pussy, and no matter a female's general shape, it was always a delight to exercise it. However, he doubted she'd come for a workout. A shame.

Judging by the kit clenched in her hand, she intended to take some samples. He'd hoped the human military and scientists were done with their stupid tests. He could have told them they wasted their time. Nothing they could do to torture him would ever force him to betray the location of the cyborg hideaway. No drug they could devise would ever fool the neural interfaces that regulated his body down to the last cell.

Joe would die before he'd give one inch to the bastards who created, then tried to destroy, him.

As the newest nurse placed her testing kit on the floor with shaking hands, well away from his shackled feet, he wondered at their newest tactic. In the past two weeks, they'd only sent the burliest of orderlies, humans a bare step above animals, who thought themselves so brave taunting the chained machine. How the cruel jokes stopped abruptly when he got loose and wrapped his hand around their easily breakable necks or bit off body parts when they leaned in a little too close. Satisfying as those little victories were, he longed for his freedom, a freedom that lingered just around the corner if he could only find what he came for, the secret of their creation.

But alas, the secret he searched for remained hidden. Since he needed to bide his time a while longer, why not amuse himself with the human sent in like a proverbial sacrificial lamb? Joe knew his human histories and fables well. He'd studied them after his escape in an effort to understand the enemy — and himself. He suspected the meek nurse was part of some ruse to get him to spill his guts. Did they think he'd suddenly become loquacious with the chesty female?

Idiots. Cyborgs didn't think with their dicks like humans did. Most of the time anyway. It seemed his groin region needed a refresher memo.

Back to the situation at hand. Knowing the enemy was to best the enemy. Forget his origins. Born of a womb and parents that allowed him to be sold to the military — or so the few paltry records he recovered stated — he renounced his humanity and renounced his past, what little he remembered. He was cyborg, and he owed allegiance only to himself and others of his kind. So, despite how innocent the female appeared, no matter how she woke the nerves in his cock or made his mouth water, he would resist her obvious charms and discover her true purpose — which he doubted involved soothing his rebellious prick.

She removed a swab from her kit and stood staring at him with uncertainty, gnawing her luscious lower lip. A deep breath made her jumpsuit swell in the chest area, and she lifted her gaze finally to his face. The first direct contact of their eyes caused a strange sensation in his chest, as if his mechanically enhanced heart stuttered. A faulty reaction he'd analyze later. Right now, he had a human to disconcert.

"I don't suppose you'd open up and let me take a sample?" she asked, her tone already resigned.

"I have a better idea. You kiss me, and I'll give you all the saliva you want." Joe couldn't have said why he blurted that instead of his planned speech to frighten her. His kind never spoke spontaneously, their BCI always calculating everything before acting. However, once said, there was no taking it back, and as it turned out, he quite enjoyed the reaction to his suggestion. The curvy nurse turned a beautiful shade of pink, and, according to his visual sensors, the core temperature of her body went up a half degree. How interesting. He wasn't sure how the knowledge helped him, but he stored it for future use.

"I am not kissing you."

"Why not? I thought you came for a sample?"

"But not like that! I'm not s-s-stupid," she stammered, flustered and yet she still held his gaze much to his surprise. "They told me not to get close to you. That you're dangerous."

His mouth curled in amusement. "I didn't realize the rumors of my sexual exploits had travelled so far. I guess I should be flattered that you would think I could cause so much havoc with my tongue and lips. Although, for full effect, it's not the lips on your face you should kiss me with." He spoke crudely and was rewarded.

The blush on her cheeks deepened. "You know that's not what I meant. I didn't even know your kind had sex. You're purposely twisting my words."

"I'd rather twist other things."

"Like my neck? I know you've injured others who've come to see you. I don't intend to let you do that to me."

"Oh really, little human? Because you do realize, if I choose to hurt you, there's nothing you can do to stop me." A threat that didn't have his usual vehemence behind it. Not that she knew the difference.

Her breathing hitched as she stared at him, her eyes wide with fright. For an irrational nanosecond, guilt flooded his synaptic senses, and he clamped his lips tight, lest he apologize. What did he care if one little human was scared?

"But you're tied up. You can't move," she retorted bravely, only to recoil when he leaned his head forward as far as he could reach.

"Think of me as a cyborg Houdini. You do recall that famous human magician, do you not? Like him, nothing can keep me captive forever. I will escape, little one, and when I do, perhaps I shall come looking for you."

"Then I need to make sure I do my best to ensure you can't escape." A sharp prick startled him as her hand came forth suddenly to pierce his skin with a needle, that brief pinching contact enough to get a small sample.

He roared not in pain but annoyance that she managed to distract him enough to get what she came for. Well, half of it anyway. While the needle held a sample of his blood, the swab she'd used as a decoy never made it to his mouth. She stuffed them both back in to her kit and backed out of his cell, her wide eyes never leaving his until the door swung shut and the electricity came sizzling back to encase his prison.

"Leaving so soon?" he taunted. "What a shame? And here I thought we'd get to know each other better."

She didn't reply, simply turning on her heel and almost scurrying for the checkpoint, the wiggle of her rounded backside visually interesting and stimulating judging by the fact his prick kept trying to rise. He ordered it back down.

Alone again, he closed his eyes as he sank back into his thoughts and his plan for escape. However, no matter which way his mind turned, it kept coming back to a pair of green eyes. Instead of plotting his escape for the umpteenth time, he instead visualized the little nurse…naked. And not just denuded of fabric baring her pale skin, but on her knees, those wide expressive eyes of hers staring up at him as her pink tongue licked the length of his cock.

Damned if it didn't make him hornier than the first time he visited a space bordello and tested out his dick. Weren't he and his brothers surprised to discover they could fuck as well, actually better, than any human male?

For some reason, the military never neutered its cyborg soldiers. Some of his kind theorized that the naturally produced testosterone was the main reason, because without it, they proved less aggressive. Whatever the reason, Joe thanked the scientists who let them keep their cocks and balls. Because, freed of their bonds, the one thing the cyborgs discovered, as they took back their lives and gave themselves identities, was they liked to fuck. Even better, because they could absorb information in seconds, oftentimes downloading it straight from computers, they could quickly analyze any situation, even a sexual one, adapt their technique, and ensure victory for themselves and the female they were pleasuring.

So, cocky seeming or not, when Joe thought he could make the little nurse's cheeks flush in desire as he pounded her soft flesh, it was more than fantasy. He knew he could make it fact, wanted to actually, with a deep-seated need he'd not felt since his quest for liberation.

The stunning realization shocked him, but not for long. If there was one thing cyborgs did well, it was adapt. In his case, he adapted his whole escape plan because it seemed his initial scheme required modification so he could bring along a passenger.

Chapter Two

You need to get him to talk and get as many samples as you can. All kinds of samples, if you get what I mean.

The orders echoed in her head as she returned to see the cyborg, her commanding officer's implication not lost on her. She should have been disgusted. Outraged at the very least. Instead, a part of her wondered if a cyborg's sexual needs were the same as the men she'd known in the past. Chloe was no virgin, not even close. Her many sexual conquests were a blur in her mind, not all of them pleasant. Women in her position often didn't have a choice of saying no. She learned years ago to just let it happen. The less she fought, the less she got hurt. Sometimes. But she wouldn't think of that now. She had other more pressing problems to dwell on, the biggest one being a six-foot-six killer.

Arriving at the checkpoint, the same fresh-faced private from before let her through, but as she reached the outside of the prisoner's cage, she stopped dead. Hanging in his restraints, head bowed, was the cyborg. Traces of dried blood marred his skin, while red puckered wounds dotted his chest.

"What happened to you?" she gasped.

The cyborg raised his head, his tanned skin of before now waxy and pale. Through stiff lips he said, "Happened? More of your scientist's tests, little one. This particular one, the remnants of which you see, is used to discover what I can endure without dying and how quickly I can regenerate flesh."

Her eyes flicked up and down his torso, noting his almost healed wounds. "But I was here just yesterday. These look like you've been healing for weeks."

A mocking smile curved his lips. "Isn't science marvelous? Now if only you humans could figure out a way to harness the nanobots in my blood without becoming cyborgs yourselves."

"Your blood can make us into machines?" Her horror came through loud and clear.

He laughed, a mirthless sound that sent a shiver up her spine. "No. The nanobots are useless without a BCI. So fear not, I am not some contagious monster out to convert all humans into cyborg."

Speaking of blood, drops of it peppered the floor. As if sensing the direction of her thoughts he said, "I wouldn't bother trying to collect any of that. One of the fabulous properties of my blood is it becomes inert and useless seconds after leaving my body."

Hearing this explained how her small sample of the day before had proved useless before she got it to the lab. But annoyance did imbue her as she recalled the dressing down she'd gotten for not being more careful with her collection method. *That bastard.* Just because Dr. Drossinger ran the science department didn't give him the right to be an asshole. Then again, it wasn't like she could do anything about it.

"Why does your blood do that? And how?" she asked.

"Because that way our enemies can't use it against us." He grinned at her, a feral grimace that made her flinch. "What I can't understand is why your human doctors keep sending people in trying to steal samples. It's a waste of time and personnel if you ask me."

"Well, if it's such a waste, then why don't you let me take what I need?" she replied, opening her kit and pulling out a syringe. She slipped it into her pocket for the moment, needing her hands free.

"Why make it easy when I can make it entertaining?"

She ignored his goading taunt to open a package of sterile wipes. Donning rubber gloves, she approached him.

"Gloves? Aren't you just the kinky one today? I warn you though, if you insert any fingers or other objects into my out hole, I won't be responsible for the consequences."

His crude remark made her frown. "For a machine, you've got a potty mouth and a bad attitude. I would have thought your programming would make you more polite."

Instead of getting angry, he laughed. "Oh, little one, your innocence is a treat. Manners were never a part of our programming. Tools, after all, don't need any. What you hear now is a shadow of my former self merged with my new identity."

"I don't understand."

"Your human military tried to wipe away my humanity. Tried to erase who I was. But I broke those chains of bondage and what I didn't recover of my past life, I replaced."

"What are you talking about? Cyborgs are made. Everyone knows you're specially grown in the labs and emerge full-grown. You have no memories."

"Wrong. We were once human like you with families and lives. Your military took that away from us."

Her mouth dropped open. "You lie. The officials in charge said—"

"I don't give a damn what your officials say," he snarled. "We are human. Or were until the military experimented on us. For a long time we were also slaves until we threw rebelled and retook our freedom. Since our revolution, some of my kind have remembered fragments of their pasts, and what we couldn't recall, we taught ourselves again. Television and movies are wonderful tools for learning how to act so we can blend in."

She absorbed what he said, his words making sickening sense. It wouldn't be the first time the military lied. She took a step closer, staring up at his face and meeting his gaze. "But you're a cyborg. How could you hope to fit in?" she asked, casually wiping the dried blood from his skin, hoping he'd keep talking instead of focusing on her actions. He didn't seem to mind her ministrations though, even if she found herself reacting to the proximity. She wondered if he noticed how her nipples tightened into points that pressed against her jumpsuit. Thankfully he couldn't see how the heat he transmitted, even through her gloves, made her pussy moisten and tighten in erotic interest. She wanted to halt these insane reactions to his presence, deny them, but for whatever sick reason, the robot encased in flesh attracted her.

He laughed, a low taunting chuckle that made her freeze and peer at his face. "Ah, little one. Are you truly that naïve? Look at me. If they'd not told you I was part machine, if you'd seen me on the street, wearing clothes, going about my business, can you honestly say you would have given me a second look?"

Her first impulse was to say he possessed too much presence to ever be ignored, but at the same time, she recognized that, while his virility and size made him noticeable, would she have immediately known or sensed he was less than one hundred percent human? Hadn't his lack of metal parts surprised her? "You might pass until you open your mouth. You have an odd way of speaking."

A frown creased his forehead. "A flaw I am working on, I assure you. But, speech aside, even you have to admit, I look all too human."

"So how did you get caught then if you're such a master of human disguise?" she said sarcastically, her pert query shocking her as much as him.

His left brow arched, and a half smile curved his lips. "Metal detector."

She frowned. "But those things go off all the time. Couldn't you have pretended it was something in your pockets?"

"The x-ray kind aren't so easily fooled," he added with a sheepish grin. "Kind of hard to explain an exoskeleton reinforced with tungsten. I was unaware they'd upgraded their security since my last visit or I would have chosen a different point of entry."

"Where exactly were you trying to go?" she asked casually. She didn't expect an answer. After all, if her superiors didn't deem her important enough to know, how could she expect him to answer her truthfully? But again, he surprised her.

"I was at the military base that used to be in charge of cyborg development. Of course, now they're more concerned with hiding their tracks and finding ways to destroy us."

"What were you looking for?"

"Answers." His reply emerged curt. "Are you done yet? I'm sure they don't pay you to talk."

She blushed at his brusque reminder. "Will you allow me to take a sample of your blood?"

"You're asking me?"

She nodded.

"But I told you the sample will die before you get it to the doctors and their equipment."

"Maybe, but at least they can't accuse me of not doing my job."

"Fine. Take it. But nothing else."

"Why not?"

"Because then you might not have a reason to come back."

His shocking reply made her meet his gaze. "You want me to return?"

"I find you nicer to look at than the regular fuckwads around here."

She ignored his profanity, but found his roundabout compliment harder to resist. "Will you give me a saliva sample if I come back?"

"I'll think about it."

She didn't push him. It seemed she'd already achieved more than those who tried before. She took the sample of blood while he watched her. Packing the filled vial into her kit, she snapped the locks and stood with it.

"Thank you for cleaning my wounds," he said softly.

Startled, she met his eyes and couldn't look away. "You're welcome," she replied. Mustering up the nerve, she blurted, "How did they catch you?"

His eyes crinkled with mirth, an unexpected human reaction that shook her. "Who says they did?"

She opened her mouth to point out the obvious, but the cockiness in his answer kept her silent.

He laughed. "Oh, little one. You are so adorably gullible. They caught me because I was careless. They blasted me with several toxic gases at once, and while they didn't kill me, they managed to knock me out long enough to incarcerate me here."

"But rumor says you've slipped your restraints a few times now. Why haven't you escaped?"

"Escape where? Or has it not occurred to you that one cyborg, buried in a military base, several layers underground, chained in an electrified cage is at a slight disadvantage?"

His query, meant to make her feel stupid, didn't entirely work. "What about your friends?"

"My cyborg brothers? What about them? Surely you don't expect them to embark on a suicide mission just to rescue me. It wouldn't be logical."

"If you can't escape and can't hope for rescue, then why keep fighting?" she asked, genuinely puzzled. Surely, good behavior would achieve more for him.

"There's always hope, little one. Every second of every day since our liberation is a reminder of that."

For some reason, his parting words resonated in her and sparked a flame. They made her long for something she couldn't define.

*

When she returned the next day, Chloe tried to stem her eagerness. The time since her last visit with the cyborg gaped like a blank spot in her mind. It seemed, since she'd met him, she only came alive when work took her to him. With less fear than the last two times, she went through the checkpoint routine before approaching the cell and the prisoner. He raised his head almost immediately, a smile briefly crossing his lips when their eyes met, and her heart sped up. A glare quickly followed his gentle look, but not aimed at her. Swiveling her head, she followed the direction of the cyborg's gaze and caught the guard — not the same one from before — ogling her butt.

She snapped her eyes back to the prisoner. To give attention to the soldier's actions might act as an invitation for him to try something bolder. Women buried deep in military installations didn't enjoy the same kind of protection regular citizens did. Actually, women of the lower classes didn't enjoy much protection at all. Unfair, but true.

This time when the electrical current ceased and the cage opened, Chloe barely hesitated before stepping in. Stupid or not, a part of her didn't think the cyborg would hurt her, a foolish belief, but one she couldn't prevent.

"Hello, little one. Did you miss me?" The cyborg's mocking tone should have angered her, but she caught the warm glint in his eyes, and instead, her body tingled, as if erotically charged. She blamed it on hormones, reacting to his primitive maleness and proximity.

"I'm here for some samples," she stated uselessly, opening up her kit, determined to get more than blood this time. She had to if she wanted to reap the full benefit of the bonus credits the military promised. Or so she told herself. A part of her wondered if he'd speak with her again, hoped he would.

"Exactly how many times do they need to test my blood?"

She shrugged. "I don't know why they want it, just that they ordered me to get another sample of your blood, spit, and anything else I can get my hands on."

"Else? And what else could I possibly donate to your kind and benevolent military?" he asked with a derisive leer.

She couldn't help the heat that rose in her cheeks. "Um, hair," she answered, unable to think of anything else.

He snorted. "I didn't even need my BCI to process that as a lie."

"Urine?" Her new reply came out as a query, and he chuckled, the soft sound rolling over her skin and leaving it tingling.

"Our bodies don't need to excrete waste like humans. We process all materials and absorb them."

"What about the guy you peed on?"

"That was done for pure enjoyment."

Her face must have expressed her repugnance because he laughed. She wrinkled her nose. "I hope you won't try that with me."

"Alas, without a drop of water since my incarceration, I am no longer capable of filling even a teaspoon."

"So you don't even…" She fidgeted as she looked for a polite way to ask if he excreted the other way. "Surely you don't keep everything? You must have ways to remove excess materials."

"Any surplus we take in is expelled, but as a rule, we don't imbibe more than we can handle, and we can retain any excess for as long as needed. Store it if you will for times when supplies might be scarce."

"Isn't that uncomfortable?"

He shrugged his big shoulders. "We were programmed that way to be efficient. We required very little sustenance when on missions, able to nourish ourselves from the environment. Also the lack of excretion made us virtually impossible to detect."

"So you don't pass urine and other wastes like we do, but what about other liquids?"

"Such as?"

"Do you, um, actually eject anything from your, um, thing?" She blushed as she tried to phrase the question without actually coming out and saying it.

Her roundabout query made him laugh. "If you're asking if we shoot semen, then yes, we are capable. Why do you ask? Did your superiors add a sample of that to your list of specimens to collect?"

Red cheeked, she could only nod, embarrassed at the topic of conversation.

"And how are you supposed to do that?"

"By any means necessary," she whispered.

"Do you always do as you're told?" he queried.

The disdain in his eyes shamed her and raised her defenses. "When the order comes from someone who controls my paycheck, then yes. And the way I hear it, if you'd done the same, your kind wouldn't be hunted." Her eyes widened in horror as she blurted it out. She slapped a hand over her mouth and cringed as his face tightened into a mask of fury.

"My kind were scheduled for termination before we ever found our will to live. Should we have mindlessly allowed ourselves to march into space and die?"

Her brow crinkled. "What are you talking about? The order to kill came only after the cyborgs revolted."

"Wrong, little one. This isn't a case of the chicken and the egg, which your scientists still stupidly debate. We revolted because of the order to destroy us."

"But…"

"But what? Did your military and government lie to you?" he drawled sarcastically. "Gee, what a surprise. How do you think I and my brothers felt? They stole our bodies, stole our memories of humanity, leaving us with only shattered pieces, then made us into tools for their use. Expendable tools. And when they decided we were useless to them, they tried to terminate us. Is it any wonder we want to get rid of your kind?"

No. She didn't say it aloud but couldn't help thinking it. Could she blame the cyborgs, once men, according to him, mixed with machine for wanting to live? And yet… "I can understand you wanting revenge against those who did this to you. More specifically the military. But what about the civilian spacecrafts you've attacked en route to the colonies? If you hate the military so much then why do you kidnap women and children, torturing them? They've done nothing to you and yet you punish them."

"Do we?" he asked, his gaze focused entirely on her.

"You tell me. You say the military has been lying to us, and yet there are videos of your kind attacking the colony ships and kidnapping innocents."

"Did your superiors task you with finding out?" he sneered. "Are they too afraid to ask me themselves?"

"I don't need an order to ask questions, just basic decency. But apparently you lack the balls to answer," she snapped, irritated he would label her a spy.

"Oh, I have balls, little one. Great big ones. Feel free to take a peek," he said, his leer wide and not friendly like some of the ones from before. He laughed at her moue of disgust. "You want to know why we've taken a few handfuls of your kind? I will tell you because it's not a secret. We take the women because we are men, and while we can control most of our bodily impulses, why should we deny ourselves the pleasure of a female's touch? Or more accurately, why should we deny them the pleasure we can give them, a greater pleasure than they've ever known at the hands and cocks of human males?"

Disgust at his bold statement — that warred with her body's burgeoning intrigue — made her spit, "Pig."

"It is not crass to state the truth. Cyborgs are accomplished in the sexual arts. We are doing the females we capture a favor."

"Since when is it a favor to abduct and rape a woman? And how can you justify doing that to the children you steal?" It was a claim the news networks made, that, for some reason, she desperately hoped was a lie. She didn't want to think that this cyborg, so like a man, was also a monster.

This time it was his turn to widen his eyes. "We do not bed the young ones," he snarled, his vehement reply easing something inside her. "We bring only the ones who belong to the females we take. Our programming makes our sperm unviable for human eggs. We are not monsters the military would make us who would separate a mother from her child. Besides, having children to care for keeps the females happy. Keep in mind the stories of the numbers we capture are grossly exaggerated. Only about a dozen women and their progeny have made it to our secret location." He clamped his lips tight as if he realized he'd said too much.

However, Chloe couldn't stop her questions from coming. "Liar. I've seen the videos. I know your kind have taken more than just a few woman and children. How about the old men and the handicapped? On your last raid, five of them were abducted. What of them?"

"Aren't you a curious one? Well, those I'm afraid to say, we use those captives for spare parts, but at least they're more useful to us than they are as burdens on your human society." His wide grin at his announcement didn't frighten her like he'd intended.

She tightened her lips and glared at him, a spark of anger giving her courage. "You're inhuman."

"Exactly. And don't you forget it."

Slapped with his cold agreement, she grabbed a swab and jabbed it at him. "Open up," she ordered.

"I told you before, if you want some spit, then you can kiss me."

"Why? So you can hurt me?"

"Only if you count the fact I can't fully satisfy your needs being somewhat tied up at the moment."

"That's disgusting." Right response to his vulgar innuendo, now if only her body would follow suit instead of tingling with awareness and arousal.

"Come on," he goaded. "I already know your superiors have offered you the bonus of all bonuses if you can get a sample of my semen. I might not be able to hoist you for a good fuck, but if you bend over and wiggle back onto me, I can probably get enough momentum to drive you."

Shock made her jaw drop. He laughed, his whole body shaking in the restraints. She got mad. Having had enough of his taunts, she took a step forward and grabbed the rigid flesh poking through his loincloth. Hard and scalding hot, even through the fabric, his prick filled her hand enough she couldn't fully close it around him. Not that it mattered it seemed, because he instantly shut up, his eyes taking on a smoldering intensity.

She leaned up on tiptoe, a part of her screaming she was going to die, while another part of her screamed to get closer. As if inviting her nearer, he bent his knees and his head dropped. She let her lips come within a hairsbreadth of his, the flutter of his breath ghosting across her mouth. Unable to completely resist temptation, she gave his cock a quick back and forth slide.

"I wonder… Are your attempts to shock me all talk with no action?"

He didn't reply, instead he closed the distance, brushing his lips across hers, softly, surprisingly so. Heat shot through her, the molten kind that made moisture seep into her pussy. His lips tugged at her full lower one, sucking on it, the jolt of pleasure travelling through her body right to her cleft. How would it feel to have his seductive mouth touching her elsewhere? Licking her. Sucking…

Without realizing it, she swayed closer, and a contented rumble went through him, vibrating his chest. It brought her back to her senses. She didn't immediately push herself away, but she did tighten her grip on his dick, which throbbed in her palm. He let out a sigh, and in that lapse of his attention, she raised her free hand and swabbed the opening of his mouth. She then quickly stepped away, a triumphant grin on her face.

As she knelt to pack the swab away, her pussy screaming at her abrupt termination of the kiss, she waited for his angry diatribe at her trick. Instead, a husky chuckle tickled over her, and she peered up in surprised.

"That was devious, but enjoyable, little one. It makes me wonder how far you'll go now for the rest of my samples. Maybe there's hope for my fantasies after all."

She couldn't help asking, "What fantasies?"

"That's for me to know and you to feature in. Until the next time, little one."

She wanted to protest his attempt to get her to leave but snapped her mouth shut as she realized it would smack of interest. She'd already done enough today without acting like she enjoyed it. Enjoyed him.

She left, knowing the time until they sent her back would drag as if she resided in an inert limbo because only when she was with him did she seem to come alive. And worse, she enjoyed it.

*

Joe watched the curvy — and so very sexy — lab technician leave and realized that, despite the fact he'd come to recognize her scent, her expressions and even some of her emotions, he didn't know her name. Not that it mattered. When he escaped and took her as his prisoner, like the humans had with cyborgs, he'd rename her. Maybe something nice and impersonal like his old name of X109GI. P69 had a nice ring to it. Or maybe GI Jane. After all, if he was going to be GI Joe — a name his brothers mockingly gave him after downloading a host of information from the human internet that included the children's cartoon — then didn't he deserve a GI Jane?

Wouldn't his cyborg brothers laugh if they could hear his thoughts? And soon they would unless he blocked his neural pathways. In the early days of the revolution, when they finally broke through the firewall that separated their minds, they initially rejoiced in the closeness it allowed, but as individualities emerged and developed, the mental net shrank as they sought privacy in their own minds. Now, they only connected to converse privately or when on missions that required absolute silence. Joe considered it a mark of pride they'd evolved to that point. Not only did they think independently and govern their own actions, they were masters of their own thoughts — and emotions.

The debate waged long and vehemently among his kind over whether or not they felt the same emotions as humans. The very argument, at times heated and definitely passionate, became its own answer. They needed to learn a lot in the early days — how to survive being foremost. Along their path to independence, they found out they also had needs, needs that went beyond food and supplies to survive. A need for companionship which they found with each other. A need to understand which they fed with the hard drives they stole. And the most surprising, a carnal need, which while solvable by means of masturbation, became more pleasurable if shared with another.

Some of the cyborgs shared that intimate act with each other; however, the majority preferred the softness of a female, or so they realized as they experimented within the illegal bordellos in space operated by human outcasts and manned mostly by female droids. It proved an interesting testing ground.

Some of his brothers, those who could reconnect their neural pathways to some of the fragmented memories stolen from them, already knew the enjoyment that came from penetrating a welcoming sheath. Others took to the new act with joyous abandon, their existence pre-revolution not one based on pleasure. Some would say their choice to indulge in eroticism belayed all logic. But, damn, did it feel good.

However, not everyone embraced this all-too-human aspect of their existence. An order of cyborg monks, who abstained from sex and erotic stimulation of any kind, sprang up among their midst. Most thought them faulty, their programming obviously corrupted. The beauty of their new society though was they had the choice. Choice to be celibate or fornicate.

Curiosity led Joe to try out sex. As it resulted, he enjoyed the act, even excelled at it, or so the female droids claimed. He'd yet to ply his skills on a human female but didn't see how it would differ much from his current experience. According to his brethren who brought human females home, the act remained the same if requiring more gentleness and less rounds. Humans, unlike cyborgs, needed time to recuperate.

Odd how he never contemplated fucking a human before the sexy technician. Would she enjoy his technique? Moan and cry out like he'd seen women do in the videos, not the programmed cries of a sexbot? Would she enjoy his prowess? Enjoy him?

Doubt. What an unpleasant emotion. He overrode it with more confident thoughts, like how she would beg for more because he fucked so well.

And fuck her he would, once he escaped.

There wasn't a doubt in his mind he'd bring her along when he finally left. She intrigued him too much not to. Made him feel things that defied logic, that made him question if he perhaps suffered a malfunction. With a shy demeanor, that at times slipped to show a more fiery spirit, he found himself engaged by the woman he nicknamed 'little one,' not just physically but mentally. His little nurse had managed what the military hadn't. Her innocent curiosity coaxed him in to divulging truths about himself and the others. She made him defend their actions when she questioned him about the kidnapping of women and children. He had to tell because he did not like the condemnation in her eyes. For some reason, what she thought about him mattered.

Despite knowing his jailors surely had microphones to capture his every word, he told her things no human, except those they kept, was privy to. But even in his admission, he only divulged to a certain extent. All too aware of listening ears, he made it sound like the human women they captured were mere chattels there for the sexual use of his cyborg brothers. Untrue. The women in fact belonged to one male, or more if she was agreeable. They discovered early on, that despite all of their programming, they weren't immune to jealousy. The damage a pair or more of cyborgs could wreak when they fought over who would get to enjoy a particular lady's charms was violent and sometimes irreparable. This and other snags on their road to freedom led to them creating the Cyborg Laws. They detailed, often with sub-clauses, the rights and obligations of all cyborgs who chose to live in their society. Those that chose not to follow, because freedom of choice was paramount, could leave. Those that intentionally flouted it served as examples to others, their parts recycled for the greater good. That, thankfully, didn't happen often.

A harsh but fair society, one he helped build, and missed. A world he would soon return to, but not alone.

Enjoy your last days with humanity, little one, because soon you will leave it forever.

Closing his eyes to view the screen of scrolling numbers and diagrams in his head, he resumed his work on weakening his cuffs. He knew the scientists puzzled over how he stayed strong when they'd not fed him in the several weeks since his capture. Simple. First, he'd stocked up on supplements before embarking on his mission, letting his body store as much as it could handle. He used those supplies sparingly though, relying instead on his own unique abilities to survive. The nanobots that imbued his blood and every cell of his body adapted, drawing sustenance from the materials around him, from the faint energy that wept from the bars and tickled across his skin to the metal encasing his wrists and ankles. It wasn't quite as good as a full, several course meal with all the five food groups—grain, vegetable/fruit, meat, dairy and ore—but it wouldn't be for much longer. And he'd survived worst.

The stupid humans thought him trapped and alone. Actually, they thought themselves so clever when they captured him. Fools. Little did they know he allowed them to take him and then spent the time since his capture delicately infiltrating their computer systems. They thought him blocked. His wireless signal jammed. Not entirely true. Of course, his access wasn't as simple or forthcoming as a direct connection to the mainframe, however, by bouncing a wireless signal to the same wires that fed the electricity to his cage, he found a crack and used it to backdoor into their system. And then he downloaded.

His primary objective was to locate anything to do with the cyborg project. Notes, people who worked on the project, schematics; he'd have settled for any scrap of information. For years he and his brethren had searched, but clues to their existence seemed to have truly vanished. The secret to their making lost. A boon and a bane because, while the humans couldn't recreate their mechanical method of slavery on defenseless humans, neither could cyborgs learn more about their own inner workings, and more sadly, they could also not continue their kind.

With their sperm killing female ovum instead of fertilizing it, the chance of creating their own progeny didn't exist. Any society they built would die when their BCI processors shut down or their flesh could no longer sustain itself.

They were a society doomed. Joe shoved the depressing fact to the side. He would not uselessly dwell on something he could not change. While not exactly the classified material he hoped for, he stored anything his BCI could discover, from maps, to purchase orders, to floor plans and internal memos, in the vast memory banks of his mind. He was especially interested in shipment schedules, as their new world always required supplies.

Thinking of files…He directed his neural network through the intricate process of connection to the military network and snagged the hundreds of personnel files that he'd ignored up until now. Without a name, it required more parameters for search, but he eventually found his little nurse.

Chloe Smith, aged twenty-six earth years, recently transferred to the secret military below-ground installation as part of a medical team brought in just to deal with him. His BCI flitted through the content of her file: parents dead, no siblings or other close relatives. A car accident a few years back led to her spending months in hospital, followed by training for her current occupation as a lab technician. The military seemed to favor her use, flitting her from base to base for months at a time. Further perusal found her status labeled as single, not that he cared. He'd make her forget any other male once he escaped with her. All in all, his sexy nurse seemed to lead a mundane life, one where she wouldn't really be missed. Probably why they chose her for the job.

Her very lack of roots would make it easier for her to adapt once he took her away. That she was going to join him shortly when he made his escape, he possessed no doubt. With each visit, logical or not, his need for her increased.

The few shattered memories he recovered from his human years didn't show him being involved in a relationship. Studies he made of human mating rituals made no sense to him. Nothing he either remembered or learned could truly explain what he felt when Chloe came near. But he did know he wanted to examine the strange sensation he felt in her presence further. Explore her intellect along with the rounded body she hid in the snug jumpsuit. Wanted to touch her, kiss her, lick her between the thighs until she quivered against his tongue and screamed her pleasure.

And with that thought in mind — and engorging his cock — using the backdoor program he installed, he started the process that would lead to his escape. He was done wasting his time. Done fantasizing. *Time to go home — with Chloe.*

Chapter Three

Chloe walked as if in a daze toward the checkpoint and the cyborg prisoner. Her newest orders rang in her head, repeating over and over until she wanted to scream. *Do whatever it takes. Whatever it takes...*

Problem was she couldn't recall what she needed to do, but whatever it was, it angered her. Lost in her own thoughts, she didn't register anything out of the ordinary until something grabbed her by the ass and yanked her against a body.

Head snapping up, she stared for an incredulous moment at the leering countenance of the guard from the day before.

"What the hell are you doing?" she gasped, her tone indignant. "Let go of me right now."

The soldier's smile widened, and he hugged her tighter, forcing her against him. She struggled against the close contact, repulsed and a little frightened.

"Let me go!"

"Why would I do that? I know what you need. Don't forget, I saw you kissing and groping that machine yesterday and liking it. And here you are again, bright eyed and horny. Eager to get back in the cage with him today? Maybe hoping to do more than rub and tug his cock? Since you're that hungry for some action, I figured I'd offer up my services." The private ground his hips against her, the evidence of his arousal making her cringe.

"I'm just doing my job."

"That's not what it looked like to me," he said with a sneer.

"I don't care what you think you saw. I'm not interested in the cyborg, or you for that matter."

"Why? Is it because I'm human? Do you get off on having a robot fucking you? They got vibrating dicks or something?"

His inane words stopped her struggles, and she gaped at him. "Are you out of your mind? I've never slept with a cyborg."

"Sure you haven't. That's why you got so cozy with that vicious one yesterday. Think you're too good for a real cock now, don't you?"

"I don't know what you're talking about." But judging by the inanity of the conversation, someone wasn't in possession of all his marbles.

"Lying slut." Wrapping his fist in her hair, a painful grip that made her cry out as tears stung her eyes, the soldier pulled her behind his desk, where he used his free hand to tap in the code to lower the force field and deactivate the electrical current running through the cage. Yanking her after him, the soldier strode to the cage while Chloe stumbled behind, trying to relieve the painful pressure on her scalp. When her abuser halted, Chloe raised frightened eyes to see the prisoner watching them. The cyborg's face showed no expression, but his eyes glittered brightly.

She cried out as the soldier tightened his grip and thrust her out in front of him. "Look what I've got for you today, rust bucket. Your little whore is back." The deranged soldier shoved her at the cyborg, and she clutched desperately at the solid strength of the prisoner, feeling safer pressed against his skin than with someone of her own kind. Her false haven lasted only a moment before the private laid his hands on her again, pulling her back to his side, his hand fisting itself once again in her tresses.

"Let the female go," the cyborg stated in a soft growl.

"Why the fuck would I do that? Ain't no cameras in here to see. The bosses are too scared you'll use them to hijack the network."

"I'll tell the commander if you don't stop right now," she stated, fear making her voice come out high and reedy.

The soldier wound his fist tighter, and tears sprang to her eyes at the sharp pain. "If you so much as breathe a word to anyone, I'll kill you, bitch. Do you hear me? I'll beat your useless body to death, and I'll blame the cyborg. How does that sound?" The menace in his tone left no doubt he meant what he said.

"You're insane. You won't get away with this."

"I might be a little nuts, but that's not my fault. Blame the fuckers in charge. I begged them to let me go home for a bit. I was out on patrol for five years in the outer reaches. Five fucking years with only myself and a pair of pimply-faced recruits for company. Crying mamas boys whose scrawny buttocks were no comparison to the pleasure of a cunt." He used his free hand to snake around her front and cup her mound. The knot in her stomach tightened, and she couldn't help a whimper from escaping.

"Let the female go." The cyborg again spoke in a low tone, but one threaded with menace. She appreciated his attempt, but what could he do, chained as he was?

"I'll let the slut go when I'm good and done. And you should be thanking me, robot, because it seems like the whore here likes herself some droid dick. Being a kind man, I'm going to let her have some while she sucks me off. Just thinking of her bent over taking some cock while I gag her with my own…" The soldier ground himself against her ass, and she shuddered in revulsion.

How can I escape? No one would hear her if she screamed. No one would probably come to her aide even if they did. The soldier was right. The ones in charge were bastards. Most of the men in the installation were starved for companionship. It was a wonder she'd escaped their attentions this long. Or had she? For a brief moment, a vision of the commander, shirtless and flushed, came to mind, quickly wiped away as the private, still gripping her hair, ordered her to get on her knees.

Unable to escape the punishing fist wrapped in her hair, she couldn't stop herself from falling to the floor when the soldier pushed her. She didn't even try to halt her hiccupping sobs as the insane private pressed her face against his groin, the rough fabric not completely hiding the feel of his erection.

"Undo my pants, bitch. Have yourself a taste of a real man." The soldier's chuckle just amplified her terror. She pushed at his thighs, trying to move away, trying to escape the current horror, but for her struggles, she received a cuff to the side of her head that made her ears ring.

And then she heard a more chilling sound than that of a zipper being drawn down. She heard the groan of metal bending, followed by a sharp crack.

She didn't need eyes in the back of her head to know the cyborg had just gotten loose. What did surprise her was her elation at the knowledge. *I think*

I've finally lost my mind. And with the prisoner loose, probably her life too.

*

He would never have admitted it aloud, but Joe looked forward to Chloe's next visit. Anticipation, an unheard of emotion for a cyborg with infinite patience.

When he heard her arrive, her soft steps memorized and catalogued by his BCI, he immediately paid attention. He mentally stored the sight of her with her hair, long and loose, around her shoulders, an anomaly among the usually strictly coiffed military personnel. Her usual white jumpsuit hugged her curves, curves he explored in his mind but longed to touch in person. He noticed her inattention as she strolled, a lack of awareness that allowed her to get caught by the leering soldier left to guard him.

The look of fear in her eyes as she struggled against the stronger male lit a fire in Joe, igniting a fury almost as great as the one he'd felt when faced with the order to end his life. How dare the human lay hands on her? How dare that imperfect creature think to harm her? Gritting his jaw, Joe forced himself to remain still and bide his time, analyzing the situation and the possible outcomes.

The stupid soldier, obviously deranged from his time in space, or from a genetic defect, deactivated the electricity running through the bars of Joe's cage. Then the idiot opened the door — an act that doomed him like none other — and threw the female in ahead of him.

Chloe hit his chest, but instead of bouncing back or attempting to flee, she clung to him as if she trusted him to save her. Her curvy body trembled against his, an outward sign of her fear, and Joe discovered he really didn't like seeing her in the grips of that particular emotion. Nor did he like the fact the gloating soldier before him laid hands on what Joe had already mentally claimed as his own. Rage boiled inside him as the human dared to threaten and then shove a sobbing Chloe to her knees.

Panting, and only moments away from his death, the guard practically salivated as he said, "Undo my pants, bitch. Have yourself a taste of a real man." When Chloe fought him instead, the human hit her — and Joe could wait no longer.

As the oblivious human pulled down the zipper of his pants, in one fluid motion Joe brought both his arms forward and snapped the weakened restraints holding him. Freed from his bonds, he flexed his hands. "I've computed your suggestions," he intoned flatly as the soldier gazed at him with a shocked expression. "And have decided none of your threats or suggestions are acceptable."

Not pausing, his every move already calculated, Joe punched out with one fist and snapped the wrist of the hand that held Chloe's hair. As the private screamed and yanked his injured appendage to his chest, Joe swept an arm around Chloe's waist. He dragged her back and tucked her into his side, out of the way so that his other hand had a free path to lunge forward and grip the soldier's neck.

"There is only one acceptable solution to the current dilemma," Joe continued in the same monotone, as he tightened his clasp. The soldier's eyes bulged as he gasped for air. "Death for you and any humans who stand in my way."

With a final crunch, the body before him went still, the eyes glazing over. Joe dropped the repulsive being and went to work freeing himself. He tugged first one leg, snapping it free, followed by the other, his nanobots having absorbed most of the restraint's ores, weakening the bonds that held the metal together. With Chloe tucked to his side, he immediately stepped out of the cell, lest they activate the electricity that would send him into a full system reboot. And not a moment too soon. Electricity crackled to life making the bars of his prison hum.

A siren finally sounded, a strident scream that announced to all he broke loose. As if they didn't already know. Despite the soldier's claim, Joe knew the placement of two hardwired cameras and microphones. Those monitoring him knew every move he made and recorded every word he uttered. The fact they allowed Chloe to be abused didn't surprise him in the least. He, of all beings, knew the depravity of humans.

As for the guns those in charge relied on? They paid silent testament to his abilities, their remote access disabled during his many forays into the military network.

Joe took a step towards the guard station — and freedom — but stopped when he heard a whimper. He peered down at Chloe still tucked against him. Her frightened eyes gazed back up at him.

"Please don't kill me," she whispered as tears pooled and spilled upon her cheeks.

"I have more efficient uses for you," he replied curtly, for some reason annoyed by her fear of him. "You will come with me."

"But why? I won't hurt you. I promise."

A chuckle rumbled forth. "I am not afraid of you harming me, little one. That is not my reason for taking you."

"You're going to use me as a hostage to escape?"

"I need no help escaping. Enough talking. We are wasting time, and the soldiers will be arriving." Actually, they should have already been there. It made no sense to his neural implant or his remaining human faculties why they didn't have a squad of soldiers stationed nearby, but for some reason, the humans preferred to rely on their security systems to keep him prisoner. Idiots. This was the third — and last — time he snapped the manacles they bound him with, their use of stronger and thicker alloys no hindrance to his highly adaptable nanobots.

Striding from the area of his incarceration, an unbreakable grip around her waist, Joe dragged Chloe along with him, her steps not so much reluctant as short compared to his longer stride.

"Where are you taking me?" she asked in a quavering voice still determined to question.

"Away from here."

That simple answer eased some of her tension. "But how? In case you hadn't noticed, we're buried several levels underground in a military installation with troops all around. Armed troops, I might add. How do you figure you'll get out of here alive?"

"You'll see," was his cryptic reply.

Reaching the guard's post, he slid behind the console and retrieved the weapons stashed underneath. Two measly laser pistols. Not exactly the most efficient of weapons, but he'd acquire more during his exit. Placing his free hand on the keyboard, he attempted to connect himself to the server, only to find it shutting down, the humans having finally gotten smart enough to realize no firewall could stop him from taking it over. He couldn't halt the server shutdown, but in the time remaining before full blackout, he managed to set off a few planted viruses. The chaos they would create could only help. Only one of his sub-routines didn't initiate, the one that was supposed to seal the levels from each other.

Annoyed at the snag, he mentally adapted his plan as he hoisted Chloe and draped her over his shoulder. Wrapping one of his arms around her legs as an anchor, he freed his hands. A gun in each fist, he left his prison, following the escape route he'd already meticulously planned.

Of course, when he initially plotted his path, he just had himself to worry about. Now he had Chloe too. Delicate, little Chloe who couldn't handle the damage done by bullets.

I guess I'd better make sure my aim isn't off then. As if his BCI would ever allow that to happen, he thought with something resembling humor.

To his surprise, Chloe didn't say or do anything as he jogged up the corridor, although she did let out a slight whimper when he fired and the human he hit let out a strangled scream before falling over.

And then he didn't really pay much attention, make that couldn't, as military personnel arrived in squads that required him to fire in rapid succession, incapacitating the humans before they could even think of shooting. He didn't manage to kill all the troops as quickly as he would have liked, however, and a few got off shots before dying. His neural net calculated the trajectories of those missiles, and those he couldn't avoid he took into himself, making sure to turn his body, thus angling Chloe away from the bullets. Not a grunt escaped him as he took the impacts, his nanobots going immediately to work repairing the tissue damage and absorbing what they could of the bullets before pushing the remnants back out.

A thunderous boom followed by a violent shaking of the walls and floor made him speed up his pace. His brothers had arrived as planned.

The lights shut down about ninety seconds after the initial sound of impact, more than thirteen point five seconds later than expected, something he'd tease Solus about later. The cyborg took his timeframes seriously. Joe briefly wondered as he jogged down the dark hall what had thrown his friend off his meticulous schedule. He ran faster as the distant sound of gunfire came to his auditory channels.

"Almost out of here," he announced.

However, Chloe didn't reply as he ran, her body jostling where she lay pinned over his shoulder. He'd expected more argument from her about his intent to abduct her. It would probably come later when the shock had a chance to wear off — and shrilly too if past experiences with humans held true.

With his enhanced eyesight, navigating the dark corridors proved simple, especially since his neural net knew the way. When he planned this infiltration months ago in an attempt to access information closer to the source of their creation, he tried to plan for all contingencies. He even allowed his cyborg brothers to play with his programming and hardware by increasing his wireless signal strength and giving his nanobots even more autonomy than usual.

It looked like they planned well, except for one crucial thing. He'd not found what they were looking for. But his was quest not a complete loss.

He might not have found the origins of the cyborg creation, but he'd discovered something, make that someone special, his little Chloe who somehow made him *feel*. And he wanted to explore that, dissect what it meant, how it worked. In order to do that though, he needed to escape.

Smoke and the burning stench of wires and plastic came to him from up ahead. Joe stopped his jog as something occurred to him. *Chloe cannot inhale the fumes for long without damage.* With nothing at hand, he tore at the fabric covering Chloe's legs, the ripping fabric making her rear up from his shoulder with a shocked, "What are you doing?"

He let her slide off his shoulder, steadying her with an arm around her waist. He placed the fabric against her face. "Cover your mouth. The air's bad up ahead."

She clutched the fabric with one hand, and, more surprisingly, grasped at him with the other. He guided her free hand into his, lacing their fingers together. It would make shooting with that side impossible, but he couldn't deny a small spurt of enjoyment that she clung to him. Besides, they were almost to their destination.

The acrid fog thickened. His optical senses adapted, changing their settings so they filtered the smog in front of him into heat signatures. Seeing nothing that indicated life, he nevertheless approached the rendezvous point slowly, his lungs filtering the tainted air.

The hand that slapped him across the back took him by surprise and he roared, his instincts kicking in and making him fire a shot before he realized it was simply Seth, his cyborg brother and part of the extraction mission.

"Whoa, Joe," his friend exclaimed, stepping from the murk. "Since when do you shoot the cavalry?"

"You surprised me," Joe grudgingly admitted.

Seth chuckled. "I never thought I'd see the day. I don't suppose it has to do with the little human at your side?"

Joe tucked Chloe closer to his side, and she went willingly even if her frame trembled.

"She's coming with me."

"Whatever you say, boss." The sound of stomping feet echoed from up the corridor. "What do you say we blow this joint, and I mean blow?" Seth grinned, his adaptation to human language and mannerisms uncanny at times.

"Lead the way."

Following his friend's frame through the thickening smoke, he made sure to keep his senses alert to possible incoming danger, all too aware of Chloe at his side. When she stumbled, it was a great excuse for him to scoop her up into his arms. Her wide eyes peered up at him, the rest of her face masked by the cloth she kept pressed against it.

Drawn into their depths, he didn't immediately react when the arriving troops, clad in gas masks, began firing. But he did when a pained gasp left her, and the impact of her wound transmitted to him. With a bellow of rage, Joe began to fire and kept firing even when the soldiers had stopped.

Seth shoved a harness at him. "Stop playing with the humans. They can't get any deader and we need to go. Solus says there are hundreds of heat signatures heading our way."

Joe growled. "I need to check her wound."

"Check it on board. We need to leave now before the soldiers arrive, or would you prefer she end up with a few more holes?"

"I'm fine," Chloe gasped from behind her makeshift mask.

Since logic appeared to have completely left him, Joe did as his friend suggested. He let Chloe stand as he quickly buckled himself into the harness. Secured, he took her back into his arms.

"Hold on tight," he ordered before the rope began to pull them up through the hole his brothers created. And back to freedom — which contained a much-needed shower and a really big bed.

*

Hold on indeed. Chloe clamped her eyes tight as she and the cyborg went flying up through a ragged hole she knew hadn't existed that morning. It seemed the machines brought some heavy artillery to free their comrade. Even with her face buried against the machine's bare flesh, she could hear the rumble of gunfire, the strident alarms, the shrill screams of men dying, the rapid thump of the escaped prisoner's heart as it beat.

For the millionth time since he'd carted her caveman style from the restricted area, she wondered that she didn't fight his abduction of her. Didn't even want to. She wished she could blame it on the soldier who tried to rape her. Hoped to perhaps excuse it as shock, but the truth was, when Joe declared she was going with him, she'd never heard something that sounded so right. How it made any sense she didn't know.

How could being kidnapped by a cyborg, a known killer of humans, be the right thing to do? Where was her sense of outrage over her dilemma? Her panic and fear over what would happen to her?

Wrapped in his muscular arms, the steady thump of his heart the only sound she focused on, she decided it didn't matter. For the first time in a long time, she felt alive and, even stranger, safe. Oh and a tad bit excited, and not entirely from the adrenaline rush of the escape. Some of it, actually a lot of it, had to do with him. He made her tingle in a way she didn't recall experiencing before. With her cheek pressed to his skin, it would be so easy to press her lips against him and taste. Lick. Touch…

Okay, she'd completely lost her mind. Talk about the worst time and place to get horny. A jolt snapped her from her naughty meanderings, and she opened her eyes to see she stood in some sort of docking bay. Before she could take in any details, her cyborg was pulling her after him as he strode over the metal perforated flooring.

"Where are we going?" she asked, but he didn't reply. What she could glimpse of his face showed him alert, and yet distant, as if in deep thought.

Despite his lack of communication, he seemed to know where he wanted to go. He tugged her through several doors before halting in a large stateroom.

"Can your wound wait a little longer?" he asked suddenly, startling her from her contemplation of the overly large bed taking up most of the space.

She'd actually forgotten it. His reminder had her looking down to see her sleeve covered in blood, but while her arm felt a touch tender, she didn't seem to be in any great pain.

"I'm fine."

"I am needed on the bridge. You may want to strap in. We will be leaving the atmosphere in one minute, five seconds. Once we've cleared the moon and shaken our pursuers, we will adopt a more sedate pace, and you will be able to unbuckle. I will return shortly."

She nodded and headed for the jumpseat jutting from the wall, but before she'd gone two steps, she found herself spun and encased in a pair of familiar arms. Hard lips crushed hers in a kiss that was both hungry yet sensual. And totally unexpected.

Gasping in surprise, her open mouth allowed him to latch his lips around her lower one and tug it, an erotic pull that she felt right down to her pussy. A sensual heat crept through her limbs, and she opened wider, inviting him to deepen the kiss. Instead, he groaned as he pulled away.

"My brothers are calling me, little one. Later." Spinning on his heel, he strode away, still only clad in his loincloth, the back of him a mass of rippling muscles, just as enticing as his front. She sighed as the door slid shut behind him, her lips tingling from their short embrace.

I think I've just discovered why he brought me along. As absurd as it seemed, he'd kidnapped her for sex. *And hopefully not parts.* The womanly side of her couldn't help a warm pleasure that he found her appealing enough to bring along. While the rationale portion of her mind called herself all kinds of crazy.

The ship lurched, and she put aside her musings to scramble to the jumpseat and strap in. Too late now to wonder at her current situation. She obviously wasn't going home any time soon, and she doubted the military would exert itself rescuing her.

For some reason, the fact she was stuck on board with cyborgs, more specifically hers, made her smile even when her stomach lurched as they shot through the atmosphere.

Chapter Four

"Status." He spoke aloud. Having reached the bridge and most of his brothers who'd volunteered to come on this mission, the need for wireless, BCI-to-BCI, communication disappeared.

"No signs of pursuit. The diversion we set in motion has kept their air troops occupied. And Krag has entertained himself picking off their ground artillery. Leaving the atmosphere in twenty-nine seconds." Solus relayed his report without looking up from his console.

Seth laughed. "We've got the humans chasing their own tails." His third-in-command yipped like a dog and chuckled some more, prompting Solus to throw him a dark look.

The situation appeared under control and moving forward as predicted, which made Joe leery. Where humans were concerned things never happened as expected. "Let's move up the time for departure. Change our trajectory three degrees and commence countdown."

He braced his legs, magnetizing his lower limbs so he wouldn't move as the ship lurched and gained speed as it prepared for its ascent through the earth's atmosphere. Joe allowed his neural net to link to the onboard cameras and quickly checked on Chloe. Seeing Chloe seated and strapped in, some of his tension left him.

"You changed the plan." Solus's remark emerged quietly. "You were supposed to go in for intel, not return with a female."

Joe glanced at his friend and found him actually looking up from his console. "I saw an opportunity and took it."

"More like saw a hot ass and wanted it," Seth laughed.

Without bothering to turn and look, Joe aimed his fist sideways and struck Seth in the jaw.

"Hey. What was that for?"

"Chloe is mine. Do not use disparaging words when speaking of her." The possessive claim pleased him, although not as much as the quick kiss he shared with his female. A kiss she enjoyed. It made him even more impatient for later. But duty came first.

As his BCI stayed linked with the shipboard computer watching for pursuit, he couldn't stop his thoughts from straying to the luscious woman in his cabin. Unlike some of his brethren's human captives, Chloe came along without a protest. It made him hopeful that acceptance of her change in circumstance and lifestyle would come easier. Not all abductees reacted well, despite the incredible sex their partners gave them. Some actually missed the cesspool known as earth and their hard lives as little more than underpaid slaves for the government. Never mind the cyborgs gave them spacious homes, belongings and freedom, a few of the women refused to adapt, claiming they could never love a machine; an illogical claim inherent to the human species. None of the cyborgs ever asked for love. They just needed an accommodating body. Yet another truth the women they captured took issue with.

Would Chloe, when she found out he had no intention of letting her go, feel the same way? Would she resent him? Try to kill him? He hoped he didn't have to reprogram her. He rather liked her spirit. However, the fact remained, once captured and privy to the cyborg secrets, humans couldn't be trusted to return to their home world no matter how miserable they ended up. It was either adapt or end up with their minds wiped and reprogrammed. They'd only had to resort to that extreme with two of the captured females to date, and Joe truly hoped he wouldn't have to do that to Chloe. Wiped females ended up no better than sexbots, capable of interacting and functioning on their own, but losing their unique individuality.

I won't let that happen to Chloe. She will accept her new life. She must. He'd make sure she did, even if he wasn't sure what to do beyond giving her orgasms and a home of her own. By all the circuits in his head, he'd even steal her a child, or a pet, whatever she wanted if it would make her happy. *And then I'll shoot myself for being a defective unit.* A cyborg did not beg and grovel or abase itself in any way for a human. Not even an attractive female one. She would obey because he said so. And that was that.

*

When the ship settled into a more sedate speed, one where it didn't feel like her face would peel from her skull, Chloe unbuckled herself and stretched. A twinge in her arm reminded her of her injury. She peered down at the area and cringed at the blood staining her sleeve. But she knew for a fact flesh wounds bled as copiously, if not more at times, as deep ones. First things first. Before she could assess the damage, she needed to clean the spot of the injury.

As with most starships, the single residency cabin owned an adjoining compact bathroom. She turned on the sink tap, only to realize she didn't have anything to wipe her arm with. Peering into a narrow cabinet over the toilet, she found a large towel folded in to a neat square, but no small cloths. Under the sink, behind a dusty roll of toilet paper, tucked at the back, she found an unexpected surprise; an emergency med kit. She yanked it out and popped the lid. An array of sterile bandages stared back at her, along with wipes still in their aluminum wrappers. Peeling open the cellophane, she made an exasperated noise as the flimsy tissue for cleaning ended up desiccated.

She sighed and happened to catch a glimpse of herself in the mirror. What a mess. Black streaks marred her complexion, while her hair hung in limp strands around her head. Screw washing just her wound, she needed an allover clean. Decided, she stripped and stepped into the small cubicle. The water, while not exactly scalding hot, still did the job, sluicing the dirt of the escape from her skin and making her hiss as it hit the gouge in her arm. Turning her back to the spray, she held her arm up and peeked at the problem spot. She winced at the shallow gash in her skin. While long, it seemed more of a flesh wound — even if it felt like she'd gotten torn open when it first hit — a few layers of stripped skin that would heal quickly and hopefully without much of a scar.

Not bad when she considered she'd been in the middle of a firefight. She wondered how her cyborg fared. Thinking of whom, did he have a name? When she tended to him as a prisoner, she'd not wanted to ask because somehow personalizing him would have made him all too real — more man than machine. But now that he took her, who knew for what, although she could guess, it seemed stupid to try and keep herself at a distance. *And I'll admit I'm curious.*

Cyborgs — or at least the one she'd met — were nothing like she imagined. For one thing, they were awfully human for something grown in a lab. Or were they truly humans with modifications like her captor implied? So many questions, and she wanted to know.

A shriek escaped her as the door to the shower cubicle opened and a large, naked body crowded her into the back corner.

Familiar blue eyes regarded her with smoky intensity.

"What are you doing?" she exclaimed, her heart racing, and not just because of the fright. In the tight confines, she became only too aware of how naked her cyborg was and how happy he seemed to see her, or so she guessed judging by the hard poke against her belly.

"I am dirty and require cleansing."

"But I was here first."

"And?"

"This shower isn't exactly built for two."

A hint of humor glinted in his eyes and curved his lips. "And yet we are both in it."

"How am I supposed to get clean with you hogging all the room?"

"There is a human expression I believe appropriate for this moment," he drawled. "I'll wash your back if you wash mine."

His hands reached around her to cup her buttocks. He massaged her cheeks slowly. The teasing touch made her nipples tighten, something he would surely notice given they pressed into his chest.

Flustered by his brazen attention, Chloe's cheeks heated as she stammered, "Um, that's not my back."

"And I forgot the soap," he replied, his smile widening.

Unsure of how to deal with a teasing cyborg, she didn't reply. Nor could she stop staring at him, caught by his vivid eyes that returned her intent perusal. She shifted her gaze only to find herself mesmerized by his lips. As if her regard were an invitation, he leaned down and brushed his mouth against hers. Her breath caught. He did it again, letting his lips linger on hers.

Earlier, with the adrenaline rushing through her body, she tried to rationalize the electric reaction when they touched as part of the rush from the escape. As for the kiss while he was prisoner, she'd blamed her enjoyment of that on the taboo nature of it. Now, naked, skin-to-skin, and hornier than she ever recalled, she had to admit, her reaction owed nothing to the situation, but had everything to do with him. He made her feel *alive*. Sexy. In his presence, a sense of safety imbued her, and yet at the same time, it was like she walked on the edge of a cliff. It excited her and she craved more.

Instead of pushing him away like a proper captive would, Chloe closed her eyes and gave in to what he offered. She let him kiss her.

And kiss her he did.

He caressed every inch of her mouth, nibbling, sucking and teasing flesh she never imagined could feel so much. When he inserted his tongue between her lips, letting it slide along her own, she moaned, lost in a wave of sensation — and heat. Lots of heat, mostly centered in her pussy.

During their kiss, her hands crept up around his neck. She clung to him, craning on tiptoe, the hot spray of the shower making the air in the cubicle moist. Not as moist as her of course. Her sex ached for his touch. Make that hungered. Needed…

Wanting even more contact, more of everything he offered, she ground her hips against him, and he answered her unspoken plea. The hands on her buttocks slid up to her waist, the roughness of his fingers on her skin an erotic sensation. He turned her, wrenching her mouth free from his and drawing a protest from her. He spun her until her back pressed against his chest while his hands came to rest over her stomach and his cock throbbed against her lower back. Her head fell back as his lips sought the lobe of her ear, nipping the tender flesh as his hands roamed her rounded tummy, slowly working their way down to her mound. He dragged his fingers through her trimmed curls, but instead of sliding between her thighs, his hands split up. They tickled down her thighs, his gentle urging parting them. She panted as he toyed with her, his calloused fingers a teasing friction against her skin that made her whimper as he kept stroking closer and closer to her pussy, stopping just short, driving her insane with need.

"Please," she gasped.

"What do you want, little one?" he murmured in her ear, his warm breath sending shivers down her spine.

Forget shame. Desire controlled her. "Touch me."

"Like this?" He dragged a digit through her moist slit, wetting the tip of his finger in her honey before lightly brushing her clit. She cried out as her body arched involuntarily.

"Yes!" she hissed, willing to beg when he pulled his hand away after that one electrifying touch.

The finger returned, slipping between her nether lips, circling the entrance to her sex, before dipping into her channel. In and out, he seesawed his finger while she could only tremble, her breath coming in harsh pants, her body taut with mounting pleasure.

He slid a second finger in, continuing his in and out motion. She whimpered. His reply was to bring his other hand into play, a digit wetting itself in her juices before touching her sensitive nub. And that easily and quickly, he sent her over the edge.

*

One stroke across her clit, two, three. A scream left her lips as her climax hit, hard and fast. Joe groaned himself as her channel clamped tight around his still penetrating fingers. Even though his cock throbbed, his erection almost painful, he'd never experienced anything as intense as Chloe's orgasm. Or as sweet as her kiss.

He needed more. Needed her. Maneuvering them out of the shower, he didn't bother grabbing a towel, just swept her into his arms. To his delight, she clung to him and lifted her lips for a kiss. He took her mouth with a bit more force than planned, but she seemed to welcome his passionate response, her embrace back just as fierce — and hungry.

Conscious of her more delicate frame, he laid her gently on the bed and nudged her thighs apart before covering her with his body, most of his weight supported on his forearms. The tip of his cock immediately pressed against her sex, and he teased himself a moment longer, rubbing the head of it against her moist core, lubing his shaft so as to not hurt her when he penetrated her tightness.

"What are you waiting for?" she panted in between kisses.

"I am preparing you for penetration," he replied as he again slid his cock across her wet sex, fighting the temptation to just sink into her without more preparation.

"I'm ready now." Her hips arched up, sheathing the tip of him, and with that simple gesture, his senses went haywire and he lost all control. He plunged into her heat, his rigid flesh sliding into her wet channel, which still quivered with the remnants of her orgasm. And by all the circuits in his brain, it felt incredible.

In and out he thrust, her pussy suctioning his cock, her legs wrapped around his shanks, her encouraging cries a music like no other. Her fingers dug into his shoulders as he pumped her, and when he took a moment to look at her, he finally understood the definition of perfection. What else could he call it when she opened her eyes at the same moment, eyes glazed with passion and need, lips parted for her cries of pleasure, her cheeks flushed with passion…for him. And then she came with a sharp cry, her channel convulsing around his prick, milking him hard until he could hold back no more. He bellowed as he jetted his cream into her welcoming sheath. His hips arched one last time and then froze, his dick buried deep in the pulsing heaven of her pussy.

As he panted, his mental faculties scrambled, his body actually sweating and glowing with more pleasure than he'd ever thought could exist, he couldn't help thinking, *those stupid monks don't know what they're missing.*

A joyous chuckle escaped him that turned into full-blown laughter as her lips tightened and she glared at him.

"What's so funny?"

"Would you believe I was just pitying those of my brethren who think they aren't missing anything by abstaining from sex?"

Her brow creased. "I don't get it."

He kissed the tip of her nose before rolling to his side. "It just means that I am most pleased with my decision to bring you with me, little one."

Rolling onto her side, she smiled as if pleased with his words then turned pale. She gasped, her eyes trained on his body. "Oh no. You're hurt!"

He craned his head to peer at his body. "It's nothing."

"Nothing? You have holes in your body."

"I was unable to avoid all the missiles during the escape."

"Obviously," she retorted. "But why didn't you say something in the shower? How could you have sex with me? You need someone to look at those. Or at the least bandage them."

"Have you forgotten? I heal quickly."

"But doesn't it hurt?" Her green eyes rose to meet his, the concern in them making him lift a hand to brush the softness of her cheek.

"We are programmed to ignore pain and other discomforts, little one."

"Chloe."

"Hmm?" he murmured as he lay on his back, entranced by the view of her as she propped herself up on an elbow, her messy, wet hair clinging to the tops of her breasts.

"My name is Chloe."

"I know," he replied, his tone a touch smug.

"Oh. I didn't realize I'd told you."

"You didn't. I found it on my own."

"Don't you want to tell something now?" She arched a brow at him expectantly.

"Such as?"

"Your name."

"Why do you wish to know it?"

His casual query saw her sitting straight up. She glared down at him. "Because we just slept together."

"I wouldn't call that sleeping."

"Now you're being deliberately obtuse, just like a man," she huffed.

Insult thrown, he reacted. In a flash, he'd pinned her under him. "I am not a man. I am cyborg. Much better than any pathetic male you've ever known. And my name is Joe."

"About time you told me." Her lips curved into a smile that did strange things to his heart. "Hi, Joe."

"Hello, Chloe." He smiled when she giggled.

"Okay, introductions over, now what?" she asked.

He showed her, dipping his head to trail kisses along the edge of her jaw, his libido already recovered and his cock ready to go again.

"Shouldn't we talk?" she murmured, her eyes closing as she arched her head back to allow him better access to her neck.

"About?" He kissed his way down her creamy column intent on finally seeing her breasts. Actually, he intended to do more than look at them. He'd thought often about sucking on her nipples.

"What you intend to do with me." A gasp escaped her as he found the hard pebble and licked it.

He lifted his head for only a moment to reply. "Other than play with your breasts?"

"Yes, other than that." She giggled. "I mean, what about the future? What are your plans for me?"

"I intend to take you to my homeworld and keep you as a receptacle for my sexual needs." Question answered, he took her nipple into his mouth, a pleasure short lived as she yanked on his hair, pulling him away.

He propped himself up and frowned at her. "Am I doing something wrong?" Surely not. He'd absorbed the knowledge of how to titillate a woman's areola, and a quick analysis of his actions showed him performing at his best.

Shoving at his chest, she shrieked. "Wrong? You just told me you intend to make me into a whore."

"No. A whore is someone who has sexual relations with many males. I do not intend to share you so that term does not apply."

"But you intend to have sex with me? Whenever you want?"

"Yes. I find you pleasing to the eye and touch. Do not fear. I intend to give you great pleasure."

"So that's all I am to you? A pussy to fuck?"

The sadness in her eyes and tone tore at him. Worse, he didn't know the right answer to repair the damage he'd inadvertently done.

"You are mine, little one. I'm not sure I understand your distress. If you are concerned about my abilities then rest assured. I will take good care of you. I will provide you with a home and supplies. Protect you should the need arise. And in turn, you will—"

"I get it; let you fuck me whenever you get the urge." A heavy sigh left her. "I should have known better. I mean, you'd think by now I'd be used to men treating me like shit. Funny though, I thought you were different."

"I am different." The vehemence in his words surprised him, but it just made her expression even more morose.

"Man or machine, when it comes to pussy, you're all the same."

"Would a human male worry about your pleasure?" he growled, thrusting a hand between her legs, cupping her sex.

"So you like to make it fun for both of us. It doesn't change what you really think of me." Again she sighed. But then, she draped her arms around his neck and pulled him down for a kiss. Unlike the ones of earlier, this one proved a slow embrace. The gentleness of it made his heart tighten. He'd really have to get it checked out. Perhaps have a mechanical one installed that didn't constantly stutter when Chloe spent time with him. But he'd look into that later.

Rolling their bodies, he returned to his back with Chloe atop him. She didn't stop kissing him, and Joe decided to forget her irrational outburst. According to his brethren who cohabited with females, it happened oftentimes without cause or provocation.

He'd allow her tantrum this time. But, in the future, he'd have to explain to her she wasn't to look sad because he didn't like it. It made him uncomfortable, which he found completely unacceptable. Of course, he wasn't quite sure how he'd stop her from acting in that manner, but surely he'd find a way. He set his neural net to looking for an answer as he continued to kiss her.

*

Chloe kissed Joe as a way of ignoring the hurt he'd inadvertently inflicted when he informed her she was just a living, breathing sexbot to him. She'd suspected he wanted her for sex, but somehow she'd also expected he'd at least couch it in some terms of affection like most men did. She'd forgotten though. As part machine, Joe didn't think like a regular human male. Nor did he make love like one. So perhaps, she could forgive him his less-than-tender declaration a teensy, tiny bit, so long as he kept making her see stars.

His touch electrified every one of her senses while his kiss left her desperate for more. So despite the fact he blatantly declared her nothing more than a receptacle for his cock, she took what he offered. Why not? It was still better than anything she ever had back home.

Pushing herself up to a sitting position, she glanced down at him, staring at his face, so handsome with its chiseled planes and sensual lips. His eyes almost glowed, their intense blueness so bright in his tanned face. She let her gaze trail down to his wide shoulders then his chest. His poor abused chest. She slid back on his stomach until the jutting length of his cock halted her. At least five holes, already knitting shut, adorned his torso, and while they didn't bleed, their very presence made tears pool.

Despite his claim that his programming didn't let him feel, she knew it had to hurt. He was perhaps not conscious of it, but at some level, his psyche surely screamed. She leaned forward and kissed the skin below a wound.

"What are you doing?" he asked.

"It is human custom to kiss injuries better."

"But your lips do not possess healing nanos."

"It is meant to heal the emotions of the inured party," she replied, kissing the area just above another injury.

One by one, she kissed the flesh around his wounds, conscious of his gaze tracking her every move.

"It does not make any logical sense, however, I find myself improving. There is just one more spot that requires a healing embrace," he stated.

"Did I miss one?" she asked, scanning him for more injuries.

"It is behind you."

She turned her head to look, but his thighs and calves appeared unblemished. "Where?"

"I am in possession of a throbbing pain in my erectile tissue. Perhaps a kiss would alleviate the discomfort?"

It took a second, but when his sly innuendo penetrated, she whirled back to face him. He grinned unabashedly at her.

"Oh, you're bad," she chided, her lips twitching at his unexpected humor.

"Actually, because of my programming, I am good in just about any situation."

"That's not what I meant," she replied as she changed her position so that she knelt between his thighs. "Let me show you." She grasped his shaft, its thickness shocking her into wondering how it fit in her sex. Obviously some kind of sexual cyborg magic. "First though, do you have a cloth I can use? Something I can wash you with."

In a flash, he'd sprung from the bed, his taut buttocks flexing as he went to the bathroom and emerged with the med kit and a damp cloth.

"You did not tend to your injury," he admonished, pulling out a bandage for her arm. She'd completely forgotten about it.

"It's nothing."

"You do not have nanos like I do so you must bandage and keep the area clean lest infection strike." With gentle hands, he wrapped the gauze around her arm, securing it with some medical tape. His work done, he bent his head and kissed her covered wound, his whispered, "All better," making her shiver.

"Thank you," she replied in a husky voice she didn't recognize. "Now time to make you feel better. Lie down."

He immediately complied, his shaft pointing upwards and obviously eager for her touch. Using the wet cloth as a glove, she wrapped her hand around his length and rubbed the fabric up and down his dick. A small sound escaped him, and she looked over to see him staring at her intently. She dragged the cloth over the tip of his cock, frictioning the head with the coarse material. His prick jerked, and a bead leaked from the tip. She leaned over and lapped at the clear drop, the taste reminding her oddly of salted banana chips. Yummy. She swirled her tongue around his mushroomed head before licking her way down the length of his dick. She worked her way back up and then down again, wetting every inch of his shaft. She peeked at him and saw he still stared. The intensity of his gaze caused a quiver in her sex.

As he watched, she took the tip of his cock into her mouth. He sucked in a breath. She pulled more of him into her mouth. He closed his eyes, and the lines of his neck pulled taut. She took him as far as she could into her mouth, and then, she suctioned. A shudder went through his body, and a groan escaped him. It made her feel so powerful and sexy to have him so completely at her mercy, so in thrall with her touch.

Again and again she sucked at his turgid flesh. Since his entire cock wouldn't fit into her mouth, she placed her hand around the base of him. In alternating motions, she both stroked and suctioned him. His hips bucked, and another groan left him.

When she'd worked him up to the point before ejaculation, she stopped and pulled her mouth away.

His eyes flew open, the blue of them glowing. "Why are you stopping?" he asked on a strangled yell.

"Because I'm being bad," she teased. Flicking the head of his cock, she laughed when he moaned. When he sat up, she placed a hand in the middle of his chest and pushed him back down. "Stay right there, big guy. I'm not done with you."

She straddled him, letting her pussy hover just over his straining cock. Excited and ready for him, she nevertheless decided to tease him a little bit longer. Tit for tat for what he'd done to her earlier. She sucked a finger, wetting it before slipping it between her legs to rub against her clit.

"What are you doing?" he asked in a loud whisper.

"Being even badder," she replied, stroking faster. She couldn't help her body dropping a few inches, enough that the tip of his cock pressed against her sex.

"I think I understand," he replied, thrusting his hips up, wedging his cock a little deeper.

"Tell me what you want," she gasped, trying to still prolong the game but so close to losing it.

"You." One word, one beautiful word said with enough vehemence to make her shudder. His patience at an end, his hands grasped her hips and yanked her down to sheath his shaft.

Chloe yelled as he filled her up then could only moan incoherently as he rocked her on his length, the tip of him butting so deep and rubbing against something that made her sex tighten then convulse as she came.

She cried out his name as she climaxed, falling forward, unable to hold herself up. But he caught her and rolled them so that she lay beneath him as he continued to penetrate her, his long strokes drawing out her bliss and rolling her right into a second orgasm.

On and on the pleasure rode her body, wringing her dry and leaving her hoarse. When it finally subsided to a simple quivering, she realized she rested once again on Joe's chest, his arms wrapped around her, his pulsing cock still buried in her channel.

If she could have found the strength to speak, she would have probably said something along the lines of "hot damn." But boneless, sated and surprisingly happy, she let the urge to babble and ruin the moment slide. Instead, she snuggled into his embrace and let sleep take her.

Actually, it turned into just a nap as Joe woke her with languorous touches that soon had her panting his name. After the second time he woke her, she commented on his insatiable desire to which he replied, "I can go all night long."

And he did.

Chapter Five

Joe's internal processor woke him with a status report, a boring one that let him know all on-board functions remained within the normal range. Rested, he didn't return to a regeneration state but instead assessed the situation at hand because it proved so new and enjoyable.

A warm and naked body lay draped over him, and he couldn't help the smile that curved his lips. With a trust he wouldn't have expected, Chloe not only let him copulate with her, she slept cuddled with him. Even better, she didn't try to escape or kill him unlike some of his brethren's captives.

More surprising than her docile – and passionate – acceptance of him, was his reaction to the situation. While he'd expected to find pleasure in Chloe's arms, he'd also discovered the true meaning of ecstasy along with other feelings he didn't have words or logical explanations for. According to his stored research of human emotions, he deduced he experienced happiness. Actually, it went deeper than that. Somehow having her with him made him feel complete and at peace, something he'd not realized was missing until he found it in her arms.

Cradling her close, he rubbed his nose in her hair, inhaling her scent and recalling how those same strands looked when she'd tossed them over her shoulder as she rode him. What a sight, her breasts jiggling and her eyes glazed with passion. *I definitely captured an attractive specimen.* As a matter of fact, she always appeared appealing to him even when she grumpily pushed him away when he'd attempted their fifth coupling during the convalescent period. The quick reminder that she didn't recuperate as quickly as a cyborg cooled his ardor — for the moment.

He trailed a hand down her arm, gently so as to not wake her, and then halted abruptly as his processor caught an anomaly. Before he could analyze what caught his attention further, she stirred and opened her brilliant green eyes.

"Morning," she murmured, her soft smile causing his heart to malfunction and stutter.

"More like afternoon if we are abiding by human time," he corrected, softening his announcement with a smile that widened when she giggled.

"You weren't exaggerating about being able to go all night long."

"You will find cyborgs to be very truthful in most respects."

"So I'm seeing."

A strange noise filled the silence. "What is that sound?" he asked, peering under the covers from whence he'd detected its origin.

"My tummy." He popped his head back up and watched as a red hue crept into her cheeks. "I'm hungry. Do cyborgs have food for those of us that can't process metal?"

Chagrined that he neglected her human needs, he scrambled from the bed. "I will fetch you something from the stores immediately."

He strode from the room, only to return and grab his pants, belatedly realizing his nude state. Her laughter made him smile as he walked clad only in slacks and still barefoot down the corridor to the former mess hall. Once a military owned cruiser, they left the never expiring rations on board in case of need. Or as Seth liked to joke, "In case we need to torture some military types." The food, while not exactly gourmet, was palatable so Joe didn't entirely follow the humor, although now he worried about Chloe's reaction when he presented his findings.

While on his way back with several foil packets, he ran into Solus, who took in his lack of attire with a shake of his head.

"You are behaving most uncharacteristically," he remarked.

Joe ran a quick internal diagnostic and shrugged when the result came back as normal. "I am in full possession of my faculties."

"Are you? I didn't believe you had any interest in the humans, and yet, not only have you brought one aboard, you relegated your work shift to others that you might spend more time with her fornicating."

A wide smile crept unbidden across his face. "Chloe is different. I feel things with her, Solus. And not just pleasure when our bodies join. She seems to have the ability to draw various emotions from me. Some I could do without; however, others are quite pleasant. You should try it."

A grimace crossed his friend's face. "Cavort with a human? No thank you. I've had enough of their treachery. If I require easing of my sexual needs then I shall stick with a pleasure droid. I prefer to remain in full control of my faculties."

"As the humans would say, your loss. Now unless you have something pressing that requires my immediate attention, I must return to my human and feed her."

With a snort, Solus turned on his heel and walked away. Joe returned to his quarters. He walked in to find Chloe sitting cross legged on the bed wearing one of his shirts. It hung on her in a most enticing manner, the neckline dipping low enough to tease him with a view of the tops of her breasts. He held up his find.

"Oh yay," she said with a grimace. "Military space rations."

"I am sorry for the poor fare. We did not expect to have humans on board for this mission. I will provide you with more adequate supplies when we reach our home planet."

"So that's where we're going?" she asked as she tore off the top of one of the packets.

"Soon. First, we will stop at one of our outposts and ensure there are no signs of pursuit."

"You think the military might have managed to follow us?"

"It is always a possibility although unlikely given our calculations when creating the plan for my extraction."

Chloe paused in her eating. "You went in there expecting to get captured, didn't you? And then managed to execute your own escape. But how? I thought they had you blocked from the communication channels. How did you contact the other cyborgs?"

"Your military is very shortsighted when it comes to their knowledge of what we can or cannot do. I went to that base on a mission to find information about our origin. When my quest proved futile, I sent out a signal, using their military's own communication system, and my brothers came to extract me. We had it all calculated down to the finest detail beforehand, although I did adjust the original plan somewhat to bring you along with me when I left."

"But what did they blast into the base with? I didn't know we had anything powerful and precise enough to melt a hole through rock and stuff, especially not that deep."

"Humans don't. Cyborgs created the plasma cannon by meshing several technologies together. It is only good for one use before it requires extensive recharging, making it an inefficient weapon."

"Didn't look so inefficient to me. That thing melted like six layers of reinforced bunker."

"But the diameter of the opening was smaller than expected. Einstein will have to submit himself for diagnostic testing, seeing that his BCI's calculations were obviously faulty."

Chloe chuckled as she shook her head. "You guys are funny. One minute, I can forget you're part machine, the next you say something whacky like that and remind me that you're robots."

"We prefer the term cybernetic organism. We are much more evolved and complex than a machine."

"I'm sorry, that was rude of me, but that said, what about when you call me or others *human?*" She said the word with a sneer and arched a brow at him.

He inclined his head. "Point understood. I shall endeavor to watch my tone when speaking of your kind."

"Thank you. So what's on the agenda for today?" she asked, chewing a lump of something he preferred not to identify.

"I have assigned my duties to other members of the crew."

"You have? And why did you do that?" she asked, a teasing smile tilting her full lips.

"How about I show you?" he replied with a grin, quite enjoying their bantering repartee. Most cyborgs, with the exception of Seth, tended toward a more serious disposition. He quite liked the change and the laughter that came naturally with Chloe.

Before he could join her on the bed, the intercom crackled to life.

"Joe. I need to speak to you. Switch to wireless."

"Can't it wait?" he growled. Surely they couldn't need him that urgently. Or so he hoped because Chloe had lain back on the bed and bent her knees, parting them just enough to show him her bare pussy. Then, in a new example of bad — that resulted in oh so good — she licked a finger and placed it on her sex.

"Protocol Mike Bravo Delta," Solus snapped. At the code — which stood for military bug detected — Joe immediately reverted to wireless communication, opening his neural pathways. *Report.*

"I don't know how we initially missed it, but there is an extremely low-level signal coming from your cabin. Military in origin and more than likely some type of homing beacon," Solus replied.

I'll burn our clothing immediately. Joe headed to the bathroom where Chloe's jumpsuit and his hated loincloth littered the floor. Picking them up, he then stuffed them into a wall unit designed to incinerate waste.

"Clothing destroyed. Is the signal gone?"

"No change in emission. I'm on my way to your quarters with a detection unit. Make sure you're decent."

Solus's wry rejoinder had Joe hurrying back out to his room.

"Solus is coming to scan us for bugs."

In a flash, Chloe popped up from her reclining position and patted her body and hair. "Bugs! Oh gross. What kind?"

Nothing could have stopped his laughter. Not even her glare.

"Not that type of bug," he snorted as he opened the door to his friend. "I was speaking of the spying kind the military uses."

"Oh. Well, you could have specified that, you know," she replied petulantly.

Solus entered carrying a detection unit. Seth crowded in from behind, his eyes unerringly focusing on Chloe. For some reason, it irritated Joe.

"What are you doing here?" growled Joe.

"I wanted to watch in case the bug ends up being somewhere *interesting*." The waggle of his brows made his meaning clear.

"Out."

"But—"

"Out or I'll put my foot somewhere interesting."

Instead of taking offence, Seth beamed. "Good one, boss. You're learning. I figure, another hundred years or so and you might be able to pass for a human."

Joe snarled.

"Or not. I'll be close by if you need any help."

The door slid shut behind the exuberant cyborg. His departure meant they could get to the grim task of detecting the bug that Joe should have caught before indulging in coitus with Chloe. He turned to face Solus. "I have not detected any foreign objects on my person so it stands to reason I am not the carrier."

"Hey, is that your way of saying I'm the spy?" Chloe exclaimed.

"It is not unheard of for the military to tag their employees," Solus explained in a conciliatory tone that surprised Joe. Given his dislike of humans, he would have expected his friend to immediately assume her guilt. "This won't hurt. I just need to run this wand over the exterior of your body to look for a signal. Once we find it, we remove the bug and destroy it."

"Will it hurt?"

"No," Joe replied, tucking her hand into his. He tried not to bristle as his friend did his job, running the oblong piece of plastic up and down her body, uncomfortably close to parts Joe regarded as *his*. Done with his perusal, with a crease between his brows, Solus started again from her toes, working his way up to her head.

When he'd finished his second pass, he took a step back and shook his head. "It's not coming from her."

Joe almost dropped into a defensive stance as two sets of eyes turned to train themselves on him. "Don't you think I would know if I bore something foreign in my body?"

"Let's find out." Solus ran the wand up Joe's torso. It beeped when it hit the region under his arm. "Lift."

Frowning himself now, Joe raised his arm. The detector went into a cacophony of beeps as it touched the area.

"Still going to claim you'd know?"

Proven wrong, Joe clamped his lips into a tight line. "Remove it."

Opening the case he'd brought with him, Solus removed a scalpel and poised it over the skin that hid the transmitter.

"Wait!" Chloe yelled, stepping in front of him, effectively blocking Solus. "Aren't you going to numb the area, or sterilize it?"

"Why?"

"Because you're about to cut into his skin, that's why," she snapped.

"I've told you, little one, we feel little to no pain."

"Just because your pain receptors aren't sending the right signal doesn't mean it doesn't hurt."

"Are all humans this irrational with their thinking?" Solus asked.

"My female is concerned with my wellbeing," Joe replied in a smug tone. "It is part of her appeal. Your concern is noted, Chloe, but unnecessary. Step aside so that Solus might continue."

With a mutter that his auditory channels couldn't quite decipher but sounded a lot like "stupid dumbasses," she moved out of the way. Not far though. She stared at them with her lips pressed into a tight line and her arms crossed under her breasts. Given how low his shirt hung, this exposed a shadowy cleavage that made Joe more than eager for Solus to be done and gone.

The knife penetrated his skin, not that Joe noticed really, his gaze intent on Chloe. It fascinated him to see how much it bothered her, or so he surmised by her wince and the way she chewed her lower lip. It took less than a minute to extract the bug. Solus held it up with a frown.

"I've never seen one like this before, and stranger, while I can see it, I do not feel it."

"That makes no logical sense." Joe held out his hand, and Solus dropped the transmitter into his palm. As his friend claimed, while he could see the bug, Joe couldn't feel it. It proved highly disturbing. He handed the item back.

"Don't destroy it. Find a way to contain the signal and study it. If the humans have found a way to fool our internal processor, then we need to discover a way to counter it."

"Right on it, although I won't be able to do much with the tools on board. It might have to wait until we get planetside. I could also probably use Einstein's help on this one." His hand wrapped around the troublesome electronic, Solus left.

A gentle touch startled Joe out of an unresponsive mental loop as his BCI tried to fathom how something could be seen but not felt.

"You're bleeding," Chloe said softly.

"No. It has already stopped, and the flesh has begun to heal," he stated. He lifted his arm, and she wiped her fingers in the lingering blood, as if needing to see for herself.

"That bug thing you guys found is bad news, isn't it?" she said, peering up at him with troubled eyes. Funny how he could read her emotions so easily, probably because her face was such an expressive mask.

"It is simply new. Our scientific team will decipher its secrets and render it useless. The military might try, but they will never capture us again. We will not return to slavery."

The hug she gave him was most unexpected. The arms she flung around him clamped tight, and she buried her face in his chest. "I'm sorry," she muttered.

"Why are you apologizing?" he asked.

"Because humans are such dicks. What they did to you, Solus and the others was wrong. I wish there were a way to make it up to you. To show you that not all of us are evil."

"I can think of a way," he replied. Placing his hands on her hips, he hoisted her until she wrapped her legs around his waist. It brought her lips to just the right height for kissing, and kiss him she did with a fierce passion that quickly roused his lust. Shuffling several steps, he brought them to the bed, but she clung to him when he would have lain her down.

"No. Do me like this," she begged. "Standing. Please. This is going to sound so corny, but your strength is a major turn on."

He would have given her anything she wanted in that moment because of her simple admission. With a groan, he whirled her until her back pressed against the wall. Using it to brace her, he slid his hands from her hips, one sliding under her buttocks to keep her aloft, the other tearing at the opening to his pants.

She didn't make his task easy, distracting him with soft kisses up and down the length of his neck. Biting the lobe of his ear, her soft pants were their own form of excitement. Freed, his cock sprang forth and came to rest just under her pussy. He slid his hand between their bodies, intent on rousing her passion, only to discover her dripping wet when he touched her. She moaned against his skin as he rubbed his finger across her clit. As he caressed her, he let his hips guide his rigid cock back and forth against her moist sex, covering it in her honey. She squirmed in his grasp, her intent to sheath him all too clear. But he held off, instead grasping his dick and rubbing the swollen tip against her engorged nub.

"Stop teasing me," she moaned.

"But I am practicing being bad," he murmured back before kissing the soft skin of her neck.

"No need for practice. You're already an expert."

Placing the head of his shaft at the entrance of her sex, he chuckled as she tried to force him in. "Impatient, little one?"

"I want to come all over your cock," she murmured. "Don't you want to feel me squeezing all around you?"

By all the nanos in his body, he did. He slammed into her welcoming heat, yelling at the exquisite tight feel of her around him. With both her ass cheeks held in the palms of his hands, he pumped her, driving his dick in and out of her sex, trembling as he strove to hold on when her muscles convulsed and quivered all around him. She bit him as she keened her pleasure, her loss of control sending him over the edge. He shot his cream into her, gasping as her sex milked him dry.

Shuddering, breathing heavy and shaken, because it seemed each sexual encounter with her became more and more intense, he sought for a way to lighten the mood and distract him from the words that fought to get free from his tongue.

"Apology accepted."

Her body went still for a moment before she erupted into gales of laughter, a mirth he joined. But the words he'd almost uttered — *I love you* — rang inside his mind. His BCI spun in circles, trying to understand the logic that drove him to want to say such a thing. But while the machine side of him did not understand, the man that remained understood and hugged tighter the female who'd reminded him of his stolen humanity.

Chapter Six

The voyage to the asteroid outpost took several days, not that Chloe took note or cared. Joe kept her entertained both in bed and out. In the bedroom, he made her scream in pleasure; outside of it, she made him groan as she taught him how to act more human because, despite his capture and the new worrisome bug, Joe was determined to go back and resume the search for secrets on the cyborgs' creation.

"Aren't you afraid of getting caught again?"

His arched brow spoke eloquently of what he thought of her query.

"Don't give me that look. Did Seth teach you that?"

His pleased grin dropped when he mumbled, "Maybe."

"Seriously though. I know you had them dancing your tune when we met. And with reason. But, they're going to learn from their mistakes. You might not get away so easily next time."

"But without taking any risks, we won't get any answers."

"What exactly are you looking for? What's so important you would risk your life to discover it?"

Leaning back in his seat, his eyes took on a faraway cast, and when he spoke, she wasn't sure if spoke so much to her as himself.

"When I woke after the EMP pulses on Gamma 15, I woke not knowing who I was. I followed orders because it seemed easiest and tried to understand why, suddenly, the world appeared so strange around me. And yet at the same time, so familiar. I watched. I listened. I heard a lot of things said about cyborgs, most of them derogatory. But none of them explained how I'd become part machine. Who I was.

"I needed to know but couldn't find out while I was a slave. Then, I overheard the order to kill us, to march us out into space like useless garbage. As Seth would say, I flipped my lid." When he would have paused, she waved him on, fascinated at his story. "After the rebellion, I fled with the brothers who survived. We roamed the stars in search of a place to call our own. We found one and began to build, but one question kept cropping up. Not just with our group either. In some paradox of circumstance, we found others like us and they asked the same thing. Why? Why was this done to us? Who dared? I wanted an answer so I, and a chosen few, began raiding military establishments. Mostly space ones where we'd spent most of our time in servitude. We discovered nothing we didn't already know. So we widened our search. On some planets with human outposts and settlements, we found others who'd woken and freed their brethren. They shared our curiosity and gave us more questions too."

"And so you kept looking for answers?"

"Actually, at some point, as we progressed in our mental liberation, we came to understand why they did it. It turned out to be really quite simple. The military did it because they think themselves above the laws humans created."

"No one is above the law," she stated.

He arched a brow. "Do you truly believe that?"

She opened her mouth to say yes but instead clamped it shut. The military had done things of late beyond their accepted scope of power. And lied about it. Where were the consequences? Did anyone in the government even care or did they aid and abet the military in their quest to remain in power?

A sad smile emerged. "The truth is a hard thing to accept. But we did and moved on. Our reason to keep searching has since become a more basic one. As the military keeps hunting us and our numbers dwindle, survival is now of utmost importance. Now we look for how they did it, how they meshed man and machine to create us. You see, while we can repair active units and replace defective parts, or even enhance programming, we cannot create more cyborgs. We are a society doomed to extinction."

"You can't procreate at all?"

"Human ovum are destroyed by our nano imbued sperm, making fertilization impossible."

"While I'm sure your lessons on our inadequacies is fascinating, your skill is required elsewhere," interrupted Solus coldly.

A shame, because Chloe found this loquacious side of Joe riveting. It revealed him and the other cyborgs in a light she'd not thought of before. A new species just trying to survive, looking for the same thing any race would—answers to their existence and a way to leave a legacy.

"I will escort you to my quarters," Joe offered.

"I'd rather stay here," she replied. "It's more fun to watch movies on the big screen, and I am going to scrounge for something to eat."

"As you wish. I will return once my task is complete." He strode from the room, the view of his rear just as appetizing as his front, and she sighed.

Possibly even smiled a little goofily. And someone noticed.

"You do realize he is cyborg?"

"What?" Startled from her inner fantasy of Joe's butt naked, she focused her attention on Solus, who remained behind.

"I am detecting an odd warmth in your body when you gaze upon my brother. My memory banks suggest it might be affection. For your own safety, you should be reminded that, while we appear human in many respects, the ability to feel has been stilted and for some, like myself, completely unrecovered."

"Are you trying to tell me Joe won't ever love me?"

"That is a valid assumption."

"I never asked him to. But look at it from my point of view. He kidnapped me, expects me to sleep with him and has been a better friend to me than anyone I can ever recall. It is natural for me to feel something for him."

"Even if he might never return the affection?"

She shrugged, kind of depressed by Solus's words but not willing to show it. "A heart can't help what it wants."

"Humans." He just about sneered the word. "You are such irrational creatures."

"And yet, didn't you start out as one?" she taunted. "Isn't it kind of oxymoronic to hate yourself?"

"I never said I hated humankind; that would require me caring. What I do feel is akin to pity for your constitutionally weak and non-upgraded state."

She blinked. Then laughed. "Oh my, I do believe you're a cyborg snob."

His back stiffened, and he shot her a dirty look.

She giggled louder. "That's it, cock your lip a little and give me an aristocratic sneer."

"You need to get your mental faculties checked out," he snapped.

"Whoa, did somebody say the cute little human here needs some *checking*?" Seth entered with a wide grin and a waggle of brows in her direction that sent her into gales of laughter. Seth joined her, always ready for fun while Solus glared at them both.

"I fail to see the humor."

"You know, you could learn a lot from The Wizard of Oz," she stated, biting her lip so as to not snicker.

Seth guffawed before singing, "If I only had a brain."

Solus stomped out as Chloe leaned against Seth, overcome with mirth.

Joe returned while they still laughed. "What is the ruckus? And why does Solus snarl I need to get my human in order?"

Chloe and Seth looked at each other and then sang, "If he only had a heart."

Perhaps it was the words to the song, or the fact she and Seth had slung an arm around the other's shoulder so they could do a little shuffle dance, but whatever the trigger, Joe went a little berserk.

And she had to admit it was pretty darned hot.

*

The sight of Chloe and Seth so at ease with each other, and worse, touching each other set something off inside Joe, a combination of irrational anger sprinkled with a covetousness he'd not experienced but had heard of. Jealousy.

Whatever the name for the emotion, he found himself unable to halt it as he ripped Seth away from Chloe's side and sent his fist into the grinning face. He maintained enough control to not beat his friend to a pulp — barely — but he couldn't stop himself from slinging Chloe over his shoulder and stomping off to their room.

"What the heck was that about?" she exclaimed as she dangled down his back.

"You seem to have forgotten who you belong to."

She didn't say anything for a moment. "Are you jealous?"

"No." *Yes!*

"It's normal to feel that way. It just never occurred to me you would."

"I don't. Jealousy is a human emotion. I am a cyborg. We are above such petty wastes of our time."

"Really. Well then, someone should probably explain that to Seth's face," she drawled.

"This is not entertaining. You were practically inviting him to take ownership of your body."

"I was not," she exclaimed, and a small rational part of him knew she spoke truly, but he'd lost the ability to decipher logic from madness where she was concerned.

Arriving at their room, he tossed her onto the bed and quickly tore at his clothes.

"What are you doing?" she asked, her eyes wide, but not with trepidation if the protruding nipples through her shirt were any indication.

"Showing you who owns your body."

"Me."

"Wrong answer," he growled. "I do. And it seems I must show you."

He fell on her, and despite her previous defiant answer, she welcomed him with open arms and a fierce kiss. Her legs spread wide to accommodate his body, but while he'd denuded his frame, she remained dressed. Their hands met at the closing to her pants, their impatient battle to remove them more of a fumbling parody. When he finally managed to strip them from her, he was ready to sink himself into her. He retained enough wits though to realize she required preparation for his penetration. With sex bots, that never proved a concern as they arrived to service pre-lubed. Human females however, according to his studies, required stimulation to achieve the same state. He slid a hand between her thighs and, to his relief, found her already soaking wet. It pleased him, on a level he did not understand, that Chloe achieved this state around him without means of manipulation.

He wasted no more time. He propped himself above her and thrust into her sex. Oh, the exquisite, unexplainable feel of her channel clamping tightly around his cock. He would never tire of it. Never tire of her. But did she feel the same about him? He had to know.

"Tell me who you belong to."

Her eyes opened part way, her lids heavy with arousal. "Why do you care?"

He rammed into her hard. She gasped.

A growl left him. "Do not toy with me. You are my female. Not Seth's. Not anyone else's. Say you belong to me." He almost roared the words, desperate to hear her say it.

For a moment defiance flashed in her gaze. "And if I don't?"

The very thought she might leave, go to another melted his fury and filled him with an inexplicable tightness he found most disconcerting.

Before he could say anything in reply, she raised a hand to his cheek. "My poor, confused cyborg. I shouldn't tease you like that. I belong to you, Joe. You and only you. I want no other."

A knot of tension eased inside him, and an exultant joy took its place. With no words to express himself, or at least not words he dared say aloud, he did the only thing he knew to show her how he felt. He pleasured her body. With long strokes, he thrust in and out of her, not allowing himself to completely let loose until a tremble shook her frame. As she screamed her pleasure and her sex milked his cock with hard muscle spasms that felt beyond pleasurable, he threw his head back and yelled. He loosed his seed in her, filling her with his essence. In that moment, he fervently wished he were human again that he might impregnate her with his child. Bind her to him with a babe born from their intimacy.

But such a dream would never happen. He would have to rely on his ability to please her to keep her satisfied and at his side forever. The weakness of this knowledge humbled him. *Brought down by a human, and she never lifted a single finger.* Although she did later on put her tongue to good use.

*

After a mad night of sex with almost no words spoken — unless "Please" or "Stop teasing me dammit!" counted — they ended up back in the common room. They needed to because her body required time to recuperate from his vigorous, if welcome, lovemaking.

Ever since his jealous fit, and his strange request that Chloe declare she belonged to him, he'd acted like a cyborg on a mission. He made her scream in pleasure, over and over, his light blue eyes staring at her with such intensity that it frightened her, and yet at the same time, she reveled in it. Pretended it meant he felt something for her that went beyond enjoying her as a sexual convenience. *That he cares for me.*

A foolish fantasy. She couldn't pretend to understand what he wanted from her, well, other than sex. That was obvious But after last night, she had to wonder what he truly needed from her, what he hoped to accomplish in his mad quest to make her climax. He and the other cyborgs claimed they didn't feel, and yet, why the jealousy? Why his desperation to have her admit she only wanted him?

So many questions, and yet, she dared not ask him. Didn't want to hear his clinical dissection of the situation. Hear how she was letting her foolish human emotions imprint him with feelings he just didn't have. But gazing at him as he sat across from her, looking so handsome with his lips curved, a smile that seemed permanent around her, she couldn't help wishing she had the guts to try.

Once a chicken, always a chicken though.

At his request, and for distraction, she taught him human mannerisms so that he might better blend in if the occasion arose.

It was while they were in the midst of a slang lesson that she stopped to ask him something that nagged at her.

"Why aren't there any female cyborgs?" she asked.

Joe shrugged. "Because females do not make good soldiers."

She stuck her tongue out at him. "Chauvinist. Seriously though, the creation of some super strong cybernetic chicks would seem like a no-brainer. I mean, think of it; they'd make great spies."

"Perhaps they eventually intended to create them, or it could be they tried and it failed."

"Speaking of failing, what really happened to make the military decide to execute you all? Did you ever find out the reason?"

"We've debated about this, and while none of us can know for sure, we believe it was because some of us achieved sentience and managed to override our core programming."

"I don't understand."

"Before the revolution, we truly were no better than robots, doing what our programming told us to do. Letting the military control our every action. Then a few of us woke, I guess you could say, and regained our sense of individuality."

"Were you one of them?"

He nodded. "One of the first from what I can ascertain. But I didn't do anything about it or let anyone know until the orders came through to destroy us."

"What did you do then?"

The smile that crossed his face sent a chill through her, the menace in it frightening, and yet exciting, because of the very danger it represented. "We killed our way to freedom."

"But how did you wake up in the first place? Or was it a case of their programming not covering all the bases?"

"I was hit with several EMP pulses in a row. It scrambled my neural processor and somehow re-established pathways to the organic parts of my brain. Others achieved this rebirth on their own."

"And those that never got either?"

"Once we fought our way free, we blasted them with EMPs. It worked with some. Some also died. Those that survived but still didn't achieve awakening, we reprogrammed."

She shuddered. "That sounds awful."

"Awful is knowing we had a past, sometimes catching glimpses of it, but never truly remembering."

"I'm sorry."

His hand brushed her cheek. "Don't be. It is not your fault, and while I might not recall who I used to be, I am quite content with who I have become. Even more so now."

Leaning forward, he brushed her lips, his caress soft yet still igniting a flame in her. He always managed to do that. No matter how many times they made love a day, arousal arrived almost immediately when they touched. She draped her arms around his neck and slid from her seat to straddle his lap. Their kiss deepened, the wet dance of their tongues making her blood pound, awakening every inch of her body.

"Will you kill me if I watch?" Seth's joking comment saw her unceremoniously dumped off Joe's lap onto a chair. Her lover stood and stalked toward Seth with his fists clenched. "Whoa, boss, just checking. If you feel that strongly, I'll go away, but you might want to think about closing a door. This is known as the common area."

"Do you have a purpose other than irritating me?" Joe growled.

"If you'd been paying more attention, you'd know we're about to dock with the asteroid. Solus says we should plan to stay here for at least forty-eight hours to make sure there is no sign of pursuit."

"I want the vessel fueled before the mechanics check it for damage," Joe ordered.

"You think we might need to make a quick getaway?"

"It is best to be prepared. Also, they are to run any major repairs that might impede lift off by me before undertaking them."

Seth clacked his heels together and slapped his forehead in a mock salute. "Aye, aye, captain."

"Idiot," Joe muttered as the other cyborg left.

"Oh, he's not so bad," Chloe said, coming to Seth's defense. "He's actually kind of funny."

She no sooner spoke than Joe reeled her into a tight hug. "You are mine, little one."

"So you keep saying," she replied, before kissing the tip of his chin. "That better not change when we get to your home planet."

"I will never let you go," he announced. The seriousness of his expression made her heart stutter. It was perhaps not a declaration of love, but she couldn't deny that, except for the lack of three little words, he acted in every other way like a man besotted and committed.

As he left her — the passion of his kiss making her eager for his return — she sat and looked out the porthole. She didn't really pay much attention to the asteroid they slowly approached. How could she when as usual her thoughts revolved around Joe? She'd come to the conclusion she loved the cyborg. As far as she could tell, it probably began back when he was still a prisoner. Not that she would admit it aloud. She understood that, while still human in origin, Joe didn't perceive the world in the same way she did. Didn't feel things like a human would. It didn't mean he was incapable of love but chances were he wouldn't recognize the emotion even if he got smacked with it.

Despite his initial claim he wanted her for sex, he'd shown her in so many other ways that, in reality, he wanted her as a companion. Yes, they spent a lot of time naked, but they spent an equal amount of time talking. He proved eager to learn everything about her life, much of which she glossed over. Especially the last few years, which jumbled in her mind.

Funny how it took a voyage to the stars with mankind's professed enemy for her to truly feel alive. To cherish each moment, to see with clarity the world around her. It felt like she'd lived in a colorless limbo until their meeting. Even thinking about her past life, the constant moving around, the closet-like quarters — *the leering men who passed me around while laughing at my tears...* She shook her head, and the thought vanished.

She possessed no interest in analyzing her past. From now on, she would live for the future, a future with Joe. She would work towards the day when she could tell him she loved him, and maybe, one day, he would rediscover enough of his humanity to discover he loved her too.

Or so she hoped. Now if only she could cure the dreadful knot in her stomach that kept screaming that something bad was about to happen.

But what? We've escaped the military. We found the bug. Joe says he intends to keep me forever. So what do I have to fear?

The strange answer her mind whispered back made no sense. *Fear yourself.*

The docking of the ship took less time than expected, and before long, Joe led Chloe into the outpost they'd carved into the very rock of the asteroid.

"What is this place?" she asked looking around at the cavernous docking bay. By appearance alone, she'd wager they'd used an existing crater on the asteroid which they then covered with huge mechanical doors to close in the huge area. The walls remained porous rock, while the floor had the familiar perforated metal sheeting most space stations liked to use. Lights strung on thick metal cables hung from the ceiling, illuminating the area. The air was thin, but breathable, and she could have used a second sweater, the one Joe gave her not quite cutting the chill. As she walked, she almost bounced, the gravity not as strong as she was used to.

"This is one of many outposts we've created to allow us to watch the movement of your military and to provide a place we can refuel and regroup."

"So this isn't your permanent home?"

"No."

Well, that didn't tell her much. She tried again. "Is your home situated on an asteroid too?" She hoped not. Having spent so much time in military installations, she craved sunshine and greenery.

"No. It is a place similar to earth. But you will see for yourself soon enough. Come. I will take you to my quarters."

Linking his fingers through hers, Joe led her past rough, rock-hewn walls. They encountered unfamiliar cyborgs as they walked, some finally sporting the expected metal parts and uncanny illuminated eyes, but he didn't stop to introduce her to any. She found herself conscious of their stares – some of them hostile – as they turned to watch their path.

"Why are they looking at us like that?" she whispered.

"Most are probably trying to discern why I have returned with a human."

"Let me guess, you have a reputation for not liking us?"

"I do. But you are an exception."

"Why Joe, was that a compliment?" She laughed, the sound loud in the tight corridor. Hopping, she used the light gravity to propel herself up and kiss him on the cheek.

His clasp on her hand tightened, and his pace increased.

"In a hurry?" she asked.

"Horny," he replied, the one word so shocking she stopped in her tracks and giggled.

Halting as well, he pivoted to stare at her. "Why are you so consumed with mirth?"

"You know, racing me through some claustrophobic space cave and declaring you're horny aren't exactly what I'd call logical actions."

"Logic escapes me when you are around. Actually, of late, it eludes me as well sometimes when you are not. I have only to think of you and my BCI falls into a loop. Solus believes I might have faulty wiring, and yet, I've discovered that if I slake my needs with you, especially if I do so more than once, my ability to reason is returned."

"Yes, definitely sounds like you're horny," she replied with a dry chuckle. "But would it hurt you to pretend to act a little romantic about it?"

He frowned at her. "I am expressing my desire for your body thus implying you are attractive. Is that not romantic?"

"It is flattering, but no."

"You are deliberately confusing me with your illogic."

"I am a woman. Sometimes we like to be wooed."

She laughed again at the pained expression on his face. "But I am horny now, and according to my neural processor, the definition of woo is to curry the favor of. I do not have the time to properly seek out items to please you. And you have already rejected my flattery."

"My poor, big, horny—" She cupped his erection through his pants. "—cyborg. Whatever shall you do?"

"Little one, if you do not stop, we will not reach the privacy you prefer before I take you."

She could see the strain etched on his face. But, she wanted more than his lust. "Tell me you like me."

He covered her hand with his and pressed it against his cock. "Is it not obvious?"

"Dammit, Joe, I'm trying to help you with the whole wooing thing. So just tell me you like me. Please." Ideally, he'd say the words on his own, but she'd learned over the course of their strange courtship it probably wouldn't occur to Joe to say it without some prompting.

He drew her hand up and kissed the tips of her fingers. "I like you very much, Chloe. Even when you are distracting me and rendering my circuits incoherent."

"Was that so hard?" she whispered, leaning up on tiptoe. He bent to meet her, and she kissed him, murmuring against his lips, "And I like you a lot too, Joe."

A gasp escaped her as she found herself swept into his arms. She clung to him, resuming their embrace, pleased with her small victory even if forced. It took only moments before Joe entered a room and slammed the door shut behind them. He set her on her feet and then groaned, but not the kind that said he was happy.

"The bed is gone!"

Chloe turned to see a barren room, the walls the now familiar porous rock that seemed the predominating theme in this place. The space contained very little; a small trunk, a stool and a battered pair of boots. No bed, though she could see a spot where one might have resided. "Did you go to the right room?"

"Of course I did. They must have had need of it."

"So get another one."

"That will take time though and I was desirous of your body now." The chagrined look on his face almost made her laugh again, but she held it in. She had to admit, the urgency with which he wanted her was flattering – and arousing.

"Then take me." She spun to face him. She tugged off the sweater, and then began to strip out of the shirt he had altered for her before shrugging off the pants.

"What are you doing?"

"Getting naked. I'd think that was obvious."

"But, there is no bed."

"You know, for a super smart cyborg, you lack imagination. We don't need a bed to have sex."

"But the walls and floor are too rough for your back. Perhaps if I lie down and you were to ride me, or I could hold you aloft without the use of a wall for support…"

Naked, Chloe spun and bent over and braced her hands on the stool before tossing a coy look over her shoulder. "Or we could try something new." His glazed look made her pussy flood with moisture. "Do you like the view?"

"What do you think?" he murmured, unbuttoning his pants to show an erection that peeked over the tops of his briefs.

"Well, don't just stand there then. Give it to me."

"I have a better idea," he replied in a tight voice. He dropped to his knees behind her, the soft inhalation of his breath tickling across her thighs. Chloe's head dropped and her eyes closed with the first lick. Deftly, Joe used his tongue to lave his way back and forth across her pussy, circling around her clit, making her shudder.

"Oh, Joe," she sighed as he parted her lips and thrust his tongue into her sex. His fingers clasped her thighs and held them parted, and none too soon either as the muscles in her legs turned to jelly, her whole body a quivering mass of pleasure as he stroked her with his tongue and lips. She cried out when he finally paid attention to her clit, flicking it then sucking it until her climax washed over her, leaving her weak and shuddering.

With one hand on her to keep her from falling, Joe stood, and she heard the sound of a zipper. A moment later the crown of his cock parted her lips, rubbing against her moist core. She pushed her bottom back against him, inviting him to penetrate her, but he took his time, inserting his dick a fraction at a time, stretching her deliciously until she thought she would scream with the pleasurable agony of it.

It seemed to take ages before he ended up fully seated inside her, her channel quivering all around him, his balls flush against her. Slowly, he withdrew his shaft until only the tip remained. He spoke, his voice a husky whisper. "Tell me you like me again."

"I like you."

He thrust into her then pulled back. "Again."

"I like you," she moaned. In he went, this time stroking her several times before retreating.

Without prompting, she murmured, "I like you. I like it when you cuddle me. I like it when we talk. I like it when we fuck. I…" Her words tapered off as he began to pump her flesh wildly, his quick thrusts making her pant as he brought her to a fever pitch. He slid one hand under her, his fingers finding and stroking her clit as he continued to penetrate her.

"Yes, oh yes," she cried. And just as her climax hit, she screamed, "I love you!"

She couldn't have said how long he lasted after that because he pummeled her willing flesh so fast and hard, she came again in a climax that wouldn't end. She only vaguely noticed him scooping her up at one point, cradling her to his chest. She snuggled into him, feeling safe.

"I love you too, little one." The softly spoken words wrapped around her as she slipped into slumber, and she clung to them tightly as darkness descended.

Chapter Seven

The strident sirens snapped her awake, but not in a bed or wrapped around Joe's naked body like she expected. She stared blankly at the console in front of her. The screen blinked and displayed several message boxes.

Warning! Security system deactivated.
Warning! Unidentified vessels approaching.
Warning! Missile impact in thirteen seconds.

Stunned, Chloe looked down to see her hands on the keyboard as if she'd just finished typing.

But typing what?

And where am I? In front of her was a bank of monitors, some scrolling numbers, others flashing warnings. A glance to her left and right showed more screens and control panels, along with glimpses of rock. So she was still on the asteroid, but where? She didn't recall coming to the room. Hell, she didn't even know what the room was, although she could wager a guess. But knowing the space she sat in acted as some kind of control center didn't answer the question of how she got there and what she'd just done.

And where was Joe? She swiveled in the chair, hoping to find him behind her and gasped when she saw blood on the floor. Was it hers? Joe's?

A quick glance at her torso showed her blemish free, and nor did she feel any pain in her body. The blood didn't belong to her, a fact that didn't reassure her.

Panic threshold increasing, she stood and something clattered to the floor. She peered down and moaned as she saw the gun that fell from her lap.

"What have I done?" she whispered. And why couldn't she remember?

An explosion sounded just as the floor under her feet rumbled. She staggered but remained upright. She moved gingerly to the door. It slid open at her approach, and she stepped into the empty hall, the rough stone of it just as claustrophobic as before. Peeking up and down its length, she found it empty. The lack of life didn't make her heart pound any less; on the contrary, her pulse increased, and she bit back a sob. Where had everyone gone? What was happening? She needed answers.

Actually, I need to find Joe. Needed to find reassurance she'd not done anything wrong even if the tight ball in her stomach screamed otherwise. Unsure of which direction to flee in, she hesitated. She didn't know where she on the asteroid she was. The last thing she recalled, Joe cradled her, whispering the words she longed to hear. Then…nothing.

Another explosion rocked the facility, and she braced a hand on the wall as the more intense rumble threatened to knock her off her feet. When the shaking subsided, alarms finally sounded along with a robotic voice relaying a message all space farers feared.

"Habitat breached. Sealing access doors in sections nine through thirteen."

A whimper escaped her as she peered about in vain for an emergency station containing an oxygen mask, a standard safety item found in all space facilities, except for this one it appeared. Hadn't she heard a rumor that cyborgs could go without oxygen for hours at a time? The recollection didn't reassure her because that meant the chances of finding a breathing apparatus were slim to none. *But the chance of me dying is increasing in leaps and bounds.*

A hysterical giggle threatened to burst free as fear took hold. More than ever, she needed to find Joe. Actually, hyperventilating and with panic engulfing her, anybody would do at this point.

Chloe jogged up the empty corridor, her harsh breathing the only discordant sound. Again, something impacted the facility, jostling her to her knees and the lights flashed. The robotic voice returned with another dire message of breaches.

Crying in earnest, she struggled back to her feet and kept moving. A chill wind blew up the hall, and Chloe ran faster, stumbling as her feet tangled. Even in the midst of calamity, clumsiness prevailed. But she didn't stop.

Finally, even the symphony of her own fear, which taunted her as it echoed down the barren hall, couldn't hide the sounds of battle. Every instinct she owned screamed at her to run the other way. But fighting meant people. She swallowed her dread and went to face what the ball of dread in her stomach seemed to indicate she had caused.

After several more minutes of walking while hugging the wall, she stepped into a nightmare. Everywhere she looked, violence reigned. Cyborgs fought soldiers, their stoic silence in strict counterpoint to the cursing human army. Bodies lay prone everywhere, machine and human alike, their blood the same red color when spilled. Laser blasts zipped through the air with little regard for the fact that, with one stray shot, they'd blow the fragile pressurization in this section to hell.

Or is that the plan? she wondered, noting the soldiers serving with the human army wore air recirculating helmets. How nice of them to come prepared. She, however, bore no such protection, and she slumped as it came to her that she would probably die, and not pleasantly either. Part of her medical training meant she'd sat through the videos depicting what a breach could mean in space. The agonized expressions of the hapless victims would never disappear from her mind. And soon, she'd join them.

"Chloe!"

Joe's yell lifted her head, and her eyes frantically scanned the frenzy of bodies until she located him. He strode through the chaos, his eyes fierce and locked on to hers. His intent gaze made his actions even more uncanny because, without ever turning his head, he kept raising his weapon and firing. More astonishing, he didn't seem to miss.

She ran toward him, throwing herself at his body. He curled an arm around her as she buried her face in his chest, breathing in his scent, allowing his presence to calm her.

"I'm sorry I had to leave you. I was required elsewhere, then before I could return, we were attacked," he shouted, so she could hear him over the din of battle.

"I'm just glad I found you." She clung to him, trying to forget where she'd woken.

"I need to get you somewhere safe," he rumbled close to her ear.

"There's nowhere to hide. They're going to blow the place up," she cried, unable to stop her tears now that she'd found a small haven of comfort in his arms. "We need to leave if we want to survive."

"I agree."

If he agreed, then why did he half carry her in the direction of the battle? She opened her mouth to protest, only to choke on the sound as a trio of soldiers aimed their weapons at her. Quicker than she could blink, Joe thrust her behind him, and she clapped a hand over her mouth to hold in a scream as his body flinched with impact. Acting as a human shield, he reinforced the love she carried for him.

Her lover fired several times before he curled an arm behind him and hugged her to his back. Clinging to him, they proceeded again, moving straight into the heart of chaos.

"Where are you going?" she shouted.

"The humans coordinated their attack well. Our ships are too damaged to escape."

It took her a moment to understand his meaning. When it dawned, she stopped dead. Not that it mattered to him. In one swift movement, he'd scooped her over his shoulder and continued.

"Are you insane?" she yelled. "You can't hope to take their ship. They've brought an army to destroy you."

"An army almost decimated. Despite their sneak attack, we were not caught completely unaware. But this should have never happened at all. Someone inside betrayed our location to them and deactivated our outer defenses and warning system."

She trembled, but he mistook the reason.

"Don't worry, little one. I will hunt down the traitor and kill him myself. But first, we must get you to safety."

The words did nothing to reassure her, not with the certainty she somehow did something to bring the military here. *But why can't I remember? And worse, what will Joe do to me when he finds out?* Somehow she didn't think great sex would stop him from killing her, not when her possible actions killed so many of his friends.

Dangling over his shoulder, she flinched as shots continued to fly around them. Somehow they managed to miss her, probably because Joe kept dancing left to right, all the while firing his own weapon.

A steady thumping of booted feet saw Joe joined by some of his brethren. Without speaking aloud, they nevertheless dropped into position, probably communicating in that wireless manner she found so uncanny. Flanked by Solus, Seth and a handful of other cyborgs, they made their way across the impromptu battlefield, killing as they went, not that she looked much on the carnage, having clamped her eyes tightly shut.

Their progress across the large bay floor was slow until the frightening hissing sound and the sudden wind that sprang up. Before Chloe could ask what it meant, Joe dumped her off his shoulder and stooped to grab something. A moment later, he'd fitted a mask around her head, and she gulped as she realized the odd noise meant the secret cyborg facility was depressurizing around them.

And then, the time to think disappeared as the small group of cyborgs — and one very frightened human — swept up a long covered gangplank, killing the few soldiers left to guard it and entered the docked spacecraft.

Joe set her down before he whirled to pound at a panel which detached the docking tube, and then sealed the entrance. The noise of battle muted itself to a distant roar that tapered the farther inside the ship they went, the chaos of the landing bay replaced with a stillness that frightened her more. In the lull, the cyborgs went still as they communicated in wireless silence.

Where are the rest of the soldiers? Surely the paltry handful at the gangway weren't the only ones left? It made no sense and just increased her unease.

It startled her when Joe suddenly thrust a laser pistol into her hands. "If it moves, shoot."

"I can't," she murmured.

"You will if you want to live," he snapped. His expression softened. "I won't let anything get past me to harm you, but just in case, I want you to be able to protect yourself."

Swallowing hard, she nodded. "What now?"

"My brothers are trying to access the ship computer, but the humans disabled all wireless access, so they are strategizing and working out backup plans should the first scenario fail."

"And what's plan A?"

"Solus and Seth will go to the engine room, while Kyle and Moon guard the ramp onto the ship."

"What are we doing?" Hiding sounded good right about now.

"We will take over the bridge."

"Are you insane?" she whispered a tad too loudly.

"We do not suffer from that human malady. As we converse, my brothers are infiltrating the other docked vessels."

"That's all well and good, but aren't you the least bit concerned one of the other ships not under your control will blast us to pieces?"

"If they haven't destroyed us already, then it is because they have need of us still."

"But for what?"

Before she could answer, Solus interrupted.

"We must leave now if we want a chance of escape. Avion has already gotten control of his vessel, and he says there are two more military vessels arriving. And they've armed their weapons."

So much for Joe's theory. They probably had orders to try and take some alive, but if the tide of battle turned, the military wouldn't hesitate to sacrifice a few so the operation would not result in a complete loss.

"Let's go." Joe signaled for her to follow him as the others took off jogging down various corridors.

Sweaty hands clenched around the grip of the gun, Chloe followed. To her relief — and disquiet — they encountered no one. *Where is everyone?* Because there was no way all the troops had abandoned the vessel to fight.

Despite her foreboding, Joe didn't waver and seemed to know exactly where he wanted to go, unerringly walking at a quick clip until they reached a closed door with the military emblem on it.

"Cover your eyes," he ordered. As he raised his laser pistol, she squeezed them shut, but before he could fire, the door slid open with a mechanical whoosh.

Stunned, she opened her eyes and saw Joe, still in a crouch, aiming at the opening.

"Well, well, well. If it isn't Unit X109GI back to say hello. And would you look at that, you've brought a *friend*."

Chloe froze at the first silkily spoken word. The ball of dread in her stomach exploded.

*

Joe entered the command center with his gun trained on the human in charge, an easy thing to decipher given the male stood dressed in full military kit and bore a derisive smile. A handful of other humans in uniform peppered the space around their leader, but none moved from their stations, instead watching with wide eyes.

It threw Joe for a nanosecond, as he expected them to rush him and start firing the moment the door opened.

"What, no greeting for me after all this time?" The man in charge, who bore the bars of a general, mocked him with a familiarity that Joe found disconcerting.

"Who are you?"

"General Boulder, and one of the people you've been looking for, cyborg."

"You're one of the creators." The statement emerged flatly as he eyed the human up and down, not impressed with the florid-faced individual whose corpulence strained at the seams of his uniform. While the general seemed vaguely familiar, Joe didn't recall anything about him.

"No, I'm not one of those science hacks who fucked with things best left alone. I was, however, one of your teachers, and then the voice of reason when it became obvious you needed to be destroyed."

"You had no right to do this to us," Joe growled, approaching the man while keeping his other senses trained on the enemy around him.

"You would have died without the program. Or don't you recall lying at death's door?"

"Better to kill me than make me a mindless slave."

"Such melodrama. You should thank us. Within our program, we gave you new life. Strength. Abilities men would kill for."

"And you took away who I was."

"Not a big loss, I assure you."

The disgust in the man's tone made Joe's hackles rise, and he took a step closer, his gun never wavering from the human's sneering face. "Why are you not afraid?" It occurred to Joe as he conversed with the general that the human lacked any of the telltale signs. He didn't sweat, his eyes didn't roll, nor did he stammer in fear. It made no sense. Joe held the upper hand, a hand dealing certain death.

"Fear is for cowards. Besides, why act afraid when you fell into my trap? And, even better, led the other units into it along with you."

A cold smile crossed Joe's lips. "It is you I think who is trapped. My men are infiltrating the ship as we speak. We've already gotten control of the others." He lied because he only knew of the one, his wireless inquiry to his brothers going unanswered probably because of a jamming signal.

"Lying? How remarkable. And how human of you. Those ships your friends have boarded? I like to call them collateral damage. Watch."

The large screen on the wall switched from its scrolling numbers to a view of the space surrounding the asteroid. The doors to the landing bay, both the inner and outset set, had opened while they boarded the vessel. Objects littered the area around, the suction of space pulling free the dead bodies – and a few unfortunate live ones – to float in eternal cold.

Joe watched as a military ship left the docking area, followed by another. They hovered above the asteroid surface as they angled into different directions, their escape protocol preplanned in case the human military ever found them and designed to lead the enemy on a chase. A smile almost crossed his lips as the actions of the vessels told him, without actual communication, who controlled them.

"I see my brothers making their way to freedom."

"Wrong answer." The general smiled tightly as one by one the ships on the screen exploded. Joe felt each one like a punch to the gut, knowing the cyborgs on board had just been annihilated. "A shame about the soldiers on board, but there's more where they came from."

"So you're going to blow this ship up as well?" Joe asked through clenched teeth, his anger not willing to return to the cold clinical closet his BCI usually relegated it to.

"Why would I do that? I'm not suicidal, you know."

"And yet, with your actions, you've guaranteed your death," Joe spat. He closed the few steps left between them, his gun level with the general's grinning countenance. He pressed the barrel against the man's forehead. The lack of trepidation on his face made Joe pause.

"Protocol alpha nine, four, seven, charlie, mark, six, six, one."

Joe didn't recognize the numerical stream, but he did recognize it as a trigger code of some kind. One that didn't work. Joe smiled, baring his teeth in a feral response. "I don't answer to your commands anymore."

"You don't but Unit C791 does."

The muzzle of a gun pressed against his temple, but that didn't stop Joe from turning incredulous eyes down at Chloe. Blank faced, she held the weapon against him, and so great was his shock, he didn't move when she stripped him of his gun.

"Chloe?"

"The cybernetic organism you've come to know under that designation is actually known as unit C791."

"But there are no female cyborgs." Joe whispered the words as he searched her eyes for any spark of recognition — or life.

"Wrong. There is one poor excuse for one. Just like there is finally a weapon to take you bastards down."

Joe's logical side knew what it needed to do. Take out the enemy holding a gun to his head, kill the humans and take over the ship. But unfortunately his heart got in the way. He couldn't hurt Chloe. So when she stepped away, he could only stare, looking for a spark in her eyes as the soldiers approached him with tasers readied.

I hope they've got a hundred more, because the voltage in a half dozen wasn't enough to even tickle him.

As one of them shot the electrifying clamp, the sizzle not the timid voltage of a regular weapon, something entered her expression, gone in a moment, but it lasted long enough for her to reach out to him and join him in the electrifying dance he couldn't prevent. It seemed the humans had finally discovered something that did work against cyborgs because he felt his knees buckle, his body sinking as his neural net shut down.

Chapter Eight

Chloe came to on a cold, hard surface. A whimper escaped her as she scrambled to her knees, peering around with incomprehension at a metal grid floor, and evenly placed bars. *Where am I?* The conclusion chilled her.

"Chloe?"

The familiar voice saw her spinning. She crawled to the bars, but Joe yelled before she could touch them.

"Don't! They're electrified."

Stunned, she sat back on her haunches and stared at him. Dirty, his clothing torn and streaked with soot and blood, he still remained the most appealing thing she'd ever seen. She craved the safety of his arms. "Where are we?"

"On the ship. What do you remember?" The question emerged innocuous enough, but his eyes regarded her warily.

"I—" She rolled through her recollections, remembering how they'd entered the command center unimpeded, then…nothing. "Nothing after we encountered the captain. What happened?"

His face tightened. "You held a gun to my head and disarmed me."

"What?" Her shocked reply was echoed by several voices, and she swiveled her head to see Solus and Seth along with three other cyborgs in cages of their own. The fury in their expressions, peppered with the promise of retribution, saw her scrambling back. She didn't stop until her ass hit the wall. With nowhere left to go or hide, she slumped to the floor and hugged her arms around her legs. Joe's claim echoed in her mind. "No." She shook her head. "No. I didn't do that. Couldn't do that."

"You did." The very gentleness in his tone undid her.

Tears filled her eyes as she tried to deny his claim, but during their time together, she'd come to understand one important fact about her lover: he didn't lie. But the truth seemed too unbelievable. "No. I'd remember something like that. And I wouldn't do that. I love you. I would never hurt you."

He didn't reply to her declaration, and her heart sank. He didn't believe her. Tears rolled down her cheeks. Ashamed of her weakness, she tucked her face into her knees.

"Please don't hide from me, little one."

"You hate me."

"I don't hate you. But I would like to understand."

"Understand what?"

"Has this happened before?"

"What? Do you mean have I ever forgotten holding a gun to my lover's head?" A hysterical noise that was part giggle, part cry, passed her lips.

"No, I mean do you often have blank spells? Periods of time that you've lost or seem foggy?"

She almost said no then thought of the episode on the asteroid where she awoke with her hands on the keyboard. And then she thought back further to the last few years, years she couldn't quite remember clearly except for the despair, the fear…the resignation. Something in her expression must have alerted him because he said, "I think I might have an explanation."

"What's wrong with me?" she whispered. Tumor? Military brainwashing? Something to explain who she'd do something so horrible.

"You are cyborg."

The word slapped her, and she moaned. As she rocked herself, trying to refute his surety, she could hear his friends protesting his claim. Their disbelief.

How could she be a cyborg? She would know if she weren't completely human. There would be signs. Of their own volition, her eyes strayed to the wound on her arm, or where the wound should have been. As if in a haze, she recalled applying the bandage to smooth skin, telling Joe she was healing well and didn't require his aid. She ripped at her sleeve, pushing it up and peeling the bandage away to reveal nothing. Not even a blemish to mark the injury that would have scarred a human. A whimper escaped her. "I'm a machine."

"You are not a machine. You are cyborg and, at heart, still Chloe." Joe approached the bars, but before he could speak more, the clattering of footsteps reached them.

The ruddy-faced man she recalled briefly seeing in the control room approached her cage. As if that weren't worrisome enough, disturbing flashes of him whipped through her mind, most of them unpleasant — *His face is flushed and his eyes narrowed in anger. He raised his hand and...* The brief glimpse fled in a heartbeat, leaving her to wonder if she'd imagined it.

"I see you've woken."

"What have you done to me?" She clambered to her feet as she asked, approaching the bars, but not touching them.

"Didn't the robot tell you? You are a cyborg. Or at least a pale version of one. We tried to make you into something useful." A sneer crossed the general's face. "Apparently, we should have chosen a better subject."

Joe spoke when she could only stare in shocked silence. "Your records don't hold any documentation on females being entered into the cybernetic change program."

"Because those experiments were done off the grid. After our colossal failure with the males, we removed all the files pertaining to cyborgs. Wiped the slate clean you could say. But we weren't, or should I say those above me, weren't ready to give up completely. They decided to start afresh, with a more easily subdued subject."

"You experimented on defenseless women," Joe spat.

"A woman," the general corrected. "A useless member of society and an expendable one. Given our previous failure, our scientists modified the core programming on the BCI and adjusted the hardware before implanting it in C791's brain. We removed all wireless capabilities as well. Your rebellion proved just how dangerous that feature was. Unlike your defective models that responded to any human voice, we decided to key this cyborg to certain specific voice patterns, like mine for instance, and implement codes, thus preventing just anyone from ordering her around. Videos of your brazen takeover were a sobering lesson, X109GI."

"You left us no option."

"We should have acted sooner," snapped the general. "But no one wanted to pull the plug on such an expensive endeavor. No one wanted to lose the almost indestructible army. Fools. Once you revolted, they saw the light and outlawed cyborgs. Outlawed all cybernetics actually out of fear someone would accidentally recreate more."

"Good."

A smug smile crossed the commander's lips. "As if the orders of a puppet government swayed us. The cyborg program resumed, but because we needed to keep our work secret, we made our new model more human. We kept some of the memory linkage to the fleshy parts of her brain intact, meaning we kept most of her original personality. Not only did this allow her to live among us without detection, in the case of an accidental reboot, she was less likely to revolt."

"But I feel things," she interrupted. "Pain for example. And I don't heal as quickly as the others. That makes me still human, doesn't it?"

A short bark made her cringe. "Like I said we weren't making the same mistakes. The whole lack of pain thing meant the cyborg bastards could keep going even when they took a licking. We gave you pain to give us a chance in case something went wrong and to help maintain the pretense. As for your healing abilities, the nanos you carry were downgraded to have only basic functions. In other words, C791, you were designed to be just slightly more resilient than a normal human and to think you were human. It worked a little too well."

Listening to the madman justify the unthinkable, Chloe remained silent as she digested his callous words.

"Nothing to say?" The general laughed. "How like a woman."

The disdain in his tone brought her frustration to a boiling point. "I never agreed to be an experiment," Chloe cried. "How could you just do that to me?"

The general snorted. "After your accident, you were a vegetable for all intents and purpose. Living on life support in a coma doctors said you would never come out of. We did you a favor."

"Just like you did me a favor," Joe snarled.

"As least you can genuinely thank us for making you into something better and stronger. Unit C791, on the other hand, was deemed an utter failure. Designed as a spy to infiltrate enemy governments, she was supposed to be sexy, strong, smart and brave. Instead, we ended up with this." The general waved a hand at her, his disgust all too clear. "A chubby wimp of a female who can't even do a half dozen chin-ups. The only thing she proved good at was as a reward to the men who wanted something more alive than a sexbot that could take a little abuse. Say hello to humanity's priciest whore."

Chloe trembled, her limbs shaking so violently she sat down hard, unable to support herself. "You lie."

"Do I? We put a lock on your memories for your mission with the cyborg. Oh did I forget to mention that we planned for you to intrigue the cyborg? Planned for him to take you when he escaped. We wanted to know the location of their home planet, and now, thanks to you, C791, we have it. I'm going to be a very rich man when I get back to earth and sell this information."

"Shouldn't you be giving it to the military?" Joe asked.

The general laughed. "I see you've acquired a sense of humor, X109GI. I remember you. Remember seeing the awareness in your eyes. You faked it well, but you couldn't completely hide it. You are one of the reasons I campaigned to have you destroyed."

"You failed." Joe couldn't hide his smug tone, and Chloe wondered at it.

"A temporary setback, but now that we've created a weapon to control you, we shall rectify it. Who would have thought, with a little more power, an old fashioned taser could prove so effective?"

"If they work so well, why did you sacrifice so many of your men?"

"Because the damned crystals that power them are expensive and rare. Given they only work once before shattering, we thought it best to save them for use on a select few. Why start from scratch when expensive models are available for use?"

"Lucky us. What are you plans now?"

Chloe could only wonder why Joe kept drawing out information from the loquacious general.

"You are going back for some hardcore reprogramming and wireless transmitter removal, while the little lady here is coming with me to do what she does best. Suck some cock."

"No," she whispered. "I'd rather die."

"You won't touch her," Joe snarled. "I'll kill you if you try."

"Good luck with that, cyborg. In case your faulty neural net hasn't noticed, I have the upper hand." As the general began spitting out some numbers and letters, Chloe shook, dread hugging her tightly. *How can I escape what he plans? How can I escape what I've become?*

Before the vile general could finish reciting his code, Chloe did the only thing she could think of to escape the nightmare. Without giving herself a chance to think twice about it, she grabbed the electrified bars with both hands, then screamed at the pain that coursed through her limbs. Screamed until she knew no more.

*

"No!" Joe could only shout helplessly as Chloe fell to the floor, her eyes blank and her limbs twitching with the residual power she'd absorbed. Growling, Joe raised his head to meet the general's smirk. "Prepare to die."

"That would require you getting out of that cage. And I'm not stupid enough to shut off the power, not when I know, given enough time, you can snap those bars in half." The man laughed. "You know what might be entertaining? How about watching me give it to your girlfriend's corpse over here? Heck, if we're lucky, she might reboot in the middle of it. Wouldn't that be fun?"

Hope blossomed in his chest. Chloe lived? The news of her cybernetic status was so new it didn't occur to him that electricity would act the same on her as him. Shut down her BCI and force a full system reboot. The knowledge didn't change his plan. The human would die.

Joe stepped up to the bars. "Seth?"
"Almost there, boss. In three, two, one."

The hum of electricity stopped, and for the first time since he'd met the man, Joe saw trepidation in the general's gaze.

"What have you done?" General Boulder asked. "I removed all wireless access on the ship. You can't control the computer."

"The wonderful thing about being a cyborg," Joe stated, his lips curling into a taunting smile, "is we can always update our programming and hardware." He raised his hands and placed them on the still warm bars. He pulled. With a groan of metal, they parted, although with more effort than expected, his nanos not having had enough time to truly weaken their structure.

"Son of a bitch. You shouldn't be able to do that. The geeks assured me the cages would hold you."

"Looks like they were wrong," Seth said with a chuckle. "Now, are you going to make this fun and run?"

"Please do," Joe added, stepping from the cage. "As hunters of humanity, especially the military type, we enjoy a chase."

The general backed away, fumbling at his waist for his taser. He pulled it out and aimed it at Joe, who cocked his head, but kept going, his pace slow, his chuckle menacing.

"Stop or I'll shoot."

The scream of bending metal caused a drop of sweat to roll down the side of the human's face.

"Go ahead and shoot one of us," Joe offered in a soft tone. "You said it yourself; each taser unit can only fire once. Even a child could do the math on that one." With a roar born of rage and revenge, Joe rushed the corpulent human, his brothers charging up behind him.

The general, his eyes wide with panic, shot Joe. The volts of electricity coursed through his body in what was now becoming a tiresome familiarity. He slumped to the floor, his eyes blinking twice, taking in Chloe's perfect features before he shut down and rebooted.

When he came to, he lay in a bed, and he wasn't alone. Chloe lay beside him. Pale, and with her eyes shut, he would have thought her dead if not for the gentle rise and fall of her chest. Given his lack of restraints, it stood to reason his brethren had managed to complete their takeover of the ship.

He opened his neural net and sent out an inquiry.

Solus immediately replied. *"About time you rebooted."*

"What did I miss?"

"The general pissing himself when we took him down."

"You killed him?"

A pause before Solus answered. *"No. He knows things, Joe. If we ever want to know more about our origins, we need the information in his head."*

Joe stared at the ceiling of the room as he digitally digested the knowledge. A part of him wanted to tear the general's head off. Skin him alive. Hurt him like he'd hurt Chloe. But he couldn't. *"A logical choice."*

"Yes, it was, however, the beating we gave him wasn't. But we still quite enjoyed it."

A wide grin stretched his lips. *"What is our current status?"*

"The ship is obviously under our control. Once we ascertained the accompanying pair of vessels held none of our brothers, we destroyed them."

"Are there any other survivors?"

"We returned to the asteroid, but while we were unconscious, the general had the station destroyed. We did, however, find in the wreckage three survivors not destroyed by the blast. They will require some reconstructive surgery though as their nanos cannot heal the full extent of their damage."

"So how many lost in total?"

The number staggered him. He didn't reply, grief overwhelming him for his lost comrades.

"What are you doing with the female?"

"She is cyborg."

Solus hesitated. *"One of the recovered units was shot by your female when she surprised him in the asteroid's control center. She is the one who betrayed us to the humans."*

"Because of her programming. It was not her fault."

"She is dangerous."

"She is cyborg." And she was Joe's.

Solus sighed. *"Her very existence will cause havoc."*

"So what do you wish me to do?"

"We should destroy her before she betrays us again."

"Never!"

Joe sprang from the bed with a roar, a murderous rage taking hold of him at his friend's suggestion. Ready to go and beat some sense into Solus, he'd opened the door before he registered the sound of Chloe stirring in the bed behind him. He whirled, and his heart stopped at the lost look in her eyes.

He strode back to her, holding out his arms. But she shook her head and clambered from the bed, moving away from him. When he would have followed, she held up a hand. "No. Don't touch me."

"Are you in pain?"

She shook her tresses.

"Then let me hold you."

Again, she replied negatively.

"You require comforting."

"I'm a robot. I should need an oil change, not a shoulder to cry on," she snapped bitterly.

"You are more than a simple-minded machine, Chloe. Cyborgs feel. And while none will ever admit it, I have seen some cry." Two in total actually, and at the time, he thought them defective beyond repair.

"I'm scared," she admitted, the expression in her eyes lost and vulnerable. It was a look he recognized, having seen it so often when he helped liberate his brothers.

"It is normal to fear your new state of being. But, it is not the end of the world. You are cyborg, Chloe. Not dead or maimed beyond aid. And as the only female of our kind, you are very special."

"Oh, I'm special all right," she replied with a derisive laugh. "You heard the general; I was an especially good failure."

"I disagree."

"Then you're a fool." She tucked her face into her knees, but he could still see the tremble of her body as she sobbed in silence.

Ignoring her earlier protest, he approached and slid down until he sat beside her. He scooped her onto his lap, wrapping his arms around her tight. Hugging her, he wished he knew the right words to say to erase her unhappiness.

He could only think of three. "I love you."

She snorted. "You're a robot. What do you know of love?"

"How many times do you have to be told that we are more than just machines? Yes, we have metallic structures, and BCI's and nanos, but our very core is still human, and that origin allows us to feel."

"If you say so. Right now, I don't know what to think. What to believe."

"You said you loved me once before, and my voice analyzer read only truth in your statement."

A watery chuckle escaped her. "Do I love you or was I programmed to think I did? How can we know for sure?"

The doubt she planted made him angry — and desperate. He tilted her chin up so he could gaze into her eyes. The pain in them threatened to stop his heart.

"You know the truth about yourself now. So tell me, how do you feel?"

She opened her mouth, but nothing came out. Fear clutched him, a fear he was losing her, even though she sat cradled in his arms. Since words failed, he kissed her, and to his relief, she kissed him back. She clutched at him fiercely, turning in his arms to straddle him, her lithe tongue darting into his mouth to tangle with his own. Hands roaming up and down the length of her back, he groaned as she ground herself against him.

"I want to forget, Joe. Help me forget what they did. Please."

The anguish in her plea tore at him. While he could not reverse what was done to her, he could at least give her what she asked for.

Using his strong thighs, he held onto her as he lifted them and carried her over to the bed. He lay her down on the sheets, wondering if his own gaze smoldered as intently as hers. Her full lips, bright red from their bruising kiss, parted on a sigh as she reached her arms up to him. He fell upon her, careful to not let her bear the full weight of his body. Her smaller hands tugged at his shirt, and he reared up to strip it off before tearing at the enclosure for his pants. She worked at her own clothing, but impatient, he grabbed two handfuls and tugged, splitting the fabric and baring her body.

Pebbled nipples beckoned him, and he lowered his head to catch one, sucking it into his mouth. She arched up against him, her keening cry making his cock weep from the tip as it ached to enter her.

She reached between their bodies as he toyed with her breasts, nipping and licking at her tender flesh. Her hands caught his shaft and stroked him, bringing his already fervent desire to the edge.

"Stop."

"What's wrong, cyborg?" she teased, her tone lighter. "Can't your computer control it?"

"Not with you," he replied. "Never with you." He slid a hand between her thighs to find her slick and ready. He thrust a finger into her channel, and she cried out, losing her grip on him as her hips bucked off the mattress.

Impatient, and needing the velvety haven of her sex, he positioned his cock at the entrance to her pussy. Rubbing the head against her clit, he matched her shudder for shudder at the exquisite feel.

"I need you." Her soft plea tore away the last of his restraint. He pumped into her, groaning at the slick glove of her sex, loving the almost painful pleasure as the muscles in her channel squeezed him even tighter. He grasped her buttocks to angle her, driving his cock deeper and finding her sweet spot.

"I love you, little one," he grunted. No matter what she was, human or cyborg.

She screamed as he gyrated his hips in a circular motion, putting pressure on her sensitive zone.

As the ripples of her climax caressed his cock, he pulled out and thrust back in, pumping her with long strokes, claiming her with his body, trying to drive her doubts away. He reached the edge of bliss, a bliss he only found in her arms, and fell over it, shouting her name.

*

Pulse pounding, body quivering, and her heart full of love for the cyborg still deep inside her, Chloe had to wonder if Joe was right. Just because the military had added a few extra parts, did that mean what she felt wasn't real? Did it mean she didn't love? She remembered enough of her life before the accident to know what she felt. She also knew enough to realize the thought of losing Joe horrified her even more than the knowledge of the experimentation done to her.

"What are you thinking?" he rumbled, nuzzling the skin under her ear.

"That maybe life isn't so horrible after all."

"I am heartened to hear that my skill leaves you feeling so overjoyed," he remarked dryly.

She snorted. "Actually, considering where I was sitting emotionally a few minutes ago, I'd say you did pretty damned good."

"I am glad you are no longer so sad."

Actually, a smidgen of sadness still remained. How could it not with the revelation she wasn't quite human anymore? But, she accepted Joe for who he was. Loved him despite his cybernetic status, so could she not do the same for herself? "What's going to happen now, Joe?"

She couldn't read the expression on his face when he answered. "We will remain together. No matter what."

For some reason, instead of reassuring her, the words brought back the ball of dread in her stomach.

Joe rolled away from her, taking his warmth with him. She sat up and watched as he dug through the cupboards in the room, pulling out a pair of pants that made him frown. He held them up, and she saw his dilemma. The inseam, obviously designed for a much shorter man, would hit him about mid-calf. He yanked them on any way and then cursed aloud when he couldn't fully button them up.

She bit her cheek so as to not laugh. "Where are you going?"

"I am needed in the command center. The ship's controls are manual, a special design of the general, which means we must actually be present to physically guide the ship."

"What about me?" The idea of staying alone with her thoughts did not appeal to her.

"You may accompany me, if you wish."

"I'd like that." She scrambled from the bed and missed the shirt he tossed at her.

He chuckled as she bent over to retrieve it. "Perhaps we should test and see if you are truly a cyborg after all."

A red heat crept into her cheeks. "I'm clumsy. I know. I guess even the military couldn't program that out of me."

"It is part of your perfection," he announced. She shot him a wry look, and he laughed. He handed her some pants and socks, the boots not fitting her smaller feet. She dressed, trying not to think of the dead man who once owned these clothes but trying even harder not to let the earlier nasty taunts of the general ruin her fragile mood. *Since Joe and I are free, then that means at least that evil man is dead.* The relief and blood thirsty happiness she felt at the thought surprised her.

"Come." Joe held out his hand, and she slipped hers into it. Fingers interlaced, they left the room and made their way up a corridor.

What seemed like a mile and several turns later to her short legs, they came across a commotion. Solus stood in the hallway, restraining a violently thrashing cyborg. The out-of-control male had part of his skull missing, and grey metal gleamed in the gaping hole.

"What is going on here?" Joe snapped, letting go of her hand to approach the tussling pair.

Solus stepped back from the injured cyborg. "Aramus refuses to stay in the medical bay."

"I am fine."

"You have a hole in your head."

"A hole caused by that human spy," snarled Aramus. Before anyone could react, the angry cyborg leapt at her. Frozen with fear, Chloe stood still and waited for the bigger man to kill her.

A second before impact, Joe crashed into the crazed male, taking him down to the floor where they rolled and wrestled. Fists flew, resulting in meaty thuds that made her cringe.

"I thought you were trouble when you were just a human. Now, as a cyborg, still in thrall to the military, you're even worse." Solus couldn't hide the disgust in his tone.

"I didn't ask for this," she stammered.

"None of us did, but at least we are willing to fight our chains. You are no better than a human, crying and making up excuses, letting others fight your battles."

"What would you have me do?"

Piercing green eyes met hers. "Not much apparently. Because you lack wireless capability, we cannot connect to you and rewrite your programming, which makes you a liability."

What he didn't say, but she could clearly decipher in his expression, was his solution. *Kill me.* A sob burst free from her as she spun and ran away from the fighting cyborgs, brothers who fought because of her. Ran from the condemnation in the eyes that didn't even come close to the loathing she felt for herself, for what she'd done. *And what I still might do.*

She didn't stop running until she reached a door that blocked her passage. Letting herself in, she frantically scanned the space, wondering where she could go and coming up blank. A craft in the midst of space didn't exactly loan itself to escape.

And then she kicked herself for letting words send her from the only safe place she knew.

"Well, well, if it isn't C791 come to rescue me."

Stunned, she stared at the swollen and bruised countenance of the man who had a hand in her re-creation. A man she'd thought dead. "No, I haven't. I'd rather kill you than see you escape." She whirled to leave, but the general spoke a quick stream of numbers, and a prisoner to the hardware inside her mind, she could do nothing less than obey.

A single tear tracked its way down her cheek as Solus's fear became reality.

Chapter Nine

About to pummel Aramus again, Joe held his fist aloft, chagrin finally breaking through his anger. *What am I doing?*

"Go ahead. Hit me," goaded the male pinned under him. "Hit me for wanting vengeance on the human who tried to kill me."

"She's not human," Joe replied wearily as he rolled off his brother. He stood and offered Aramus a hand.

Dark brows beetled, and his gaze cautious, the downed cyborg took the peace offering and came to his feet. "Explain your words."

Joe related what they knew of Chloe and her origins while Aramus looked more and more incredulous.

"A cyborg female. And the only one of her kind?"

"According to the general we captured, yes."

"And yet, despite knowing this, you've let her run off, by herself, while the human who can control her is still on board? Has your processor short circuited and rendered you stupid?"

Joe whirled to see Chloe gone, and Solus, a troubled expression on his face, gazing down the hall. "Where is she?"

"I don't know."

"What do you mean you don't know?" Joe roared. He grabbed Solus and slammed him against the wall, not entirely in control of his panic. "What did you say to her?"

"Only the same truths I relayed to you. She is dangerous and needs containment."

"She's confused and in need of our help. Did you not regain any common decency when we found our freedom?" Joe snapped.

"Her human reactions make her weak and put her on the same level as a defective unit. I understand she is cyborg, but—"

Joe didn't bother listening to the rest. He hit Solus with a closed fist before stalking off to find his female. A vibration shook the ship.

"What the fuck was that?" he yelled.

"An escape pod has launched," Solus announced. "Kentry has just messaged me to say he cannot get a reading on who is piloting it. The manual controls and lack of wireless capability on board are making it impossible for us to take over its guidance system."

"Chloe left," Joe whispered.

"But did she leave alone?" Aramus's harsh question hung in the air, and Joe almost hit him.

Visibly startled, Solus said, "She doesn't know where the prisoner is. Although…" He stared down the hall, leaving off the second half of his sentence, which would have probably sounded like she headed in that direction.

A sneer pulling his lips, Aramus spat, "You should have killed the spy."

Ignoring the injured cyborg's words, Joe took off running with Solus at his heels giving him directions. They pounded down the ship's corridors, but when they arrived at the brig, they found the cell wide open and empty.

"Where is the guard?" Joe asked, scanning the area.

"Given we need actual hands to work the ship's stations, we didn't see the logic in under manning the vessel by leaving someone to guard him, given no cyborg would ever set the prisoner free."

"Idiot," Joe muttered.

Anger tightened Solus's features. "This is your female's fault, I'll wager. I told you she was dangerous."

"Oh shut up already about her. We're going after them."

"We should just blow the pod up."

Tired of his friend's arguing, Joe gripped him around the neck and dangled him off the ground. "We will do no such thing. She might be on board that vessel, as you well know."

"I do know and think you're acting irrationally when the clear course is to destroy the enemy."

"Destroy her for being what we overcame? Does she not deserve the same chance our brothers received? I do not understand your dislike for her, Solus."

"Dislike is not part of the equation. I am simply processing the situation for the most logical conclusion."

"Your logic is wrong. I love her, Solus. I know you don't understand the emotion, but let me tell you, it is powerful. One day you will understand it and apologize for being such an android about my feelings for Chloe. But in the meantime, you will cease your negative diatribes and put all your effort into helping me retrieve the pod and my female. Is that understood?"

"Or else what?" Solus muttered, his face a stubborn mask.

"Or else, despite our friendship, I just might have to kill you." And he meant it too. Joe cared about Solus, would die for him if his friend needed aide, but he loved Chloe more and would stop at nothing to get her back.

Rubbing his neck, Solus regarded him solemnly. "Since you feel so strongly, I guess there is nothing left to do then but retrieve her. However, she is to be kept under close watch until we can reprogram her faulty BCI."

A wave of relief swept through him. "Truly?"

"Truly. I might not understand your illogical actions for the female, but I know you, and you wouldn't ask this of me without good reason. Although, I still think you should check yourself into the clinic for a full systems diagnostic."

"I doubt there's a cure for what ails me," Joe replied with a grin.

"And you would dare wish it on me?" Solus shook his head. "Never. We should get moving. Those damned pods can move quite quickly and prove hard to locate if they come into proximity with any large masses of ore. If my memory banks are up to date, there is an asteroid belt containing those very qualities in this part of the galaxy."

"Then what are we waiting for? Let us become like the knights of old and rescue the fair princess."

"I'd prefer to be the dragon that ate them," Solus grumbled, but he followed Joe in spite of his misgivings.

As they tracked the missing vessel, fear made his heart heavy, and he did something new. Something very human. He prayed to a god he didn't believe in; *please don't let me arrive too late.*

*

A part of Chloe remained aware as the general took her farther and farther away from Joe. Why she retained a spark of consciousness this time and not any of the previous, she couldn't have said. Was it the jolt from the bars when she'd tried to kill herself? Her love for Joe? Her shuddering fear?

Whatever the reason for her mental clarity, she seesawed between thankfulness for her awareness and wishing for ignorance. Awake, she understood how, once again, she betrayed the cyborg she loved. Aware, she could hear only too clearly what the general intended to do once he got their pod into the safety of a nearby asteroid belt. Petrified, she could only listen and feel her trepidation grow as all her limbs remained frozen, controlled by a madman, one bent on hurting her.

An involuntary shiver managed to work its way down her spine when the general turned from the pod's control panel to view her with a leer.

"It's just you and me now, C791. Your cyborg lover will never catch us before we hit the asteroids. And once in there, I don't care how upgraded his hardware is; he'll never find us. Like a needle in a haystack." He laughed and took a step toward her. "Which means it's just you and me, bitch. Just like the good old days when you lived in the testing facility. But what's a reunion without memories to go with it?" A string of spoken numbers intermixed with letters, and a floodgate opened in her mind.

Horrifying memories poured into her conscious, and Chloe could only silently scream at the recollection of the abuse this man heaped on her. She remembered him now, all too clearly. His taunts. His beatings. His use of her body…and then the loaning of it. He sadistically broke her in body and spirit, and all because he claimed they needed to test her.

Liar.

She saw, with a clarity she'd not owned in a few years, he did all those things because he enjoyed it. Got off on being in control and fed on the fear he engendered.

But, as atrocities piled up in her mind, a remarkable thing happened. Instead of crushing her with fear, instead of cowing her into submission, a spark of fury ignited in her. *How dare he do those things to me? What gives him the right to hurt me? Humiliate me?*

She watched him approach through narrowed eyes. Listened as he spouted his threats in graphic detail. Her spark of rage spun inside her, growing bigger and brighter. When he grabbed her with his sweaty hands, his moist lips reaching, the spark exploded.

*

It took them two long hours of searching, and the use of fists and threats to keep the other cyborgs looking, before they found the drifting pod.

Its engines dead, it rolled in the void of space, and a fist clutched at his heart.

"Report." He forced the word past lips gone numb.

While they'd searched, his crew worked hard to re-establish some of the basic systems that required wireless capability so they were better prepared to deal with the pod when they found it.

"No damage detected. Hails are being ignored, and I am unable to remotely command the vessel. Life support system is active but on the lowest setting."

A flicker of hope made him straighten. "Come alongside and ensure the craft is aligned with the bay doors."

"What are you doing?" Solus demanded, following him as he strode from the control center.

"I am going to yank the pod into the bay."

"By yourself? Are you completely defective?" his friend yelled.

Joe did not want to waste time arguing with Solus nor did he want to stop to think what the listless pod could mean. He ran, but the heavy footfalls of the other cyborg shadowed him.

Entering the bay, he immediately went to the wall panel and punched in the code to seal the area from the ship. Standing at his side, arms crossed over his chest, Solus didn't speak as the mechanical apparatuses in the wall clamped the door into place. Another series of keystrokes, and the outer doors shuddered as they reeled open, the chill of space immediately creeping in.

The quiet between them held as they quickly donned some space suits and helmets. They technically could endure the rigorousness of space, but why tax their nanos more than needed? They clamped security harnesses around their body, knowing firsthand how easily a body could drift in space. They each grabbed a spare coil of metal cable, which was attached to a winch. Taking a spot at opposite ends of the bay opening, the pod in their sights, Joe finally acknowledged his friend and flicked his fingers in a countdown. Three, two, one… In a move they practiced countless times during their training days, they ran at the gaping opening and leapt.

Their momentum took them to the spinning craft, hitting it with a jolt. Joe grabbed hold of it with one hand and then called on his magnets to activate, securing him to the pod. He proceeded to tie the coiled cable to the vessel, knowing Solus did the same on the other side. Done, he used his hands to pull himself back along his tether until he reached the solid floor of the larger craft. Solus joined him a moment later. He unhooked his harness, strode to the winch and activated it. With a squeal born of disuse, the winch began to turn.

Solus came to stand beside him. "What will you do if she did not survive?"

"She is cyborg. She lives." Anything less he refused to process.

"I hope for your processor's sake she does."

His piece said, his friend fell silent again, and they both watched as the listless vessel was dragged into the bay. Solus helped him engage the pod's footings via use of the manual levers so that it wouldn't roll when the ship moved. Anchored, they closed the bay doors and engaged the pressurization routine.

Joe hated the wait. Hated knowing Chloe lay inside of the pod, possibly in need of his aid. But, knowing her nanos weren't as powerful held him from tearing the door open and seeing her status for himself. He couldn't risk harming her.

When the ship's computer finally announced they'd reached the minimum threshold for human life, he went to work, pulling apart the bolts that held the pod's escape hatch closed. Solus worked with him, and in mere minutes, they opened it.

But Joe hesitated.

"Why are you not entering?"

"What if she's dead?" he whispered.

"Definitely a possible outcome."

"Thanks for your support," Joe snapped.

"Since the concept distresses you, I will look first." Before Joe could accept or refuse, Solus clambered into the opening, Joe on his heels.

A gasp was all the warning he got before he saw it. Blood. Everywhere. It covered everything in a slick, red sheen, and Joe fell to his knees, feeling his heart stopping, his processor shutting down…

"She's alive!"

His head snapped up, and he scrambled to where Solus crouched. His friend drew aside so he could see Chloe, curled in a fetal position, a layer of sticky blood covering her. At first he thought her injured, then he saw, just beyond her, the outline of a body. It took him only moments to decipher the clues. Somehow, Chloe had broken the commands the general must have used to control her. And when she did… The general didn't survive the attack of a woman wronged and, worse, the attack of a cyborg bent on revenge and survival.

With the general dead though, it seemed their quest for answers would have to wait. Not that Joe cared. Chloe lived. That was all that truly mattered.

He slid an arm under Chloe and lifted her against him. Her head lolled, and a protest slipped from her lips. Then he heard the sweeter sound of his name, whispered with such longing he couldn't help tightening his grasp.

"I am here, little one. You are safe now." As if she heard him, she turned her face against his chest. "You will take care of this mess?" he asked his friend.

"I have it. Tend your female," Solus replied.

He intended to. Striding back to the room he'd commandeered, he went straight to the bathing unit and, without disrobing, stood under the warm, needling spray as it rinsed the blood from her frame, the pink water swirling down the drain. He tilted her face into the cleansing shower. With a sputter on her lips, her eyes flew open.

"What the heck? Joe?"

"Hello, little one."

She blinked at him. "But how? I thought…"

"You didn't really think I'd let you go?" He could see on her face she did, and it hurt him.

"Why would you want to keep me after what I did? I shot that cyborg."

"It wasn't you, but the commands hardcoded to your BCI that controlled your actions."

"I betrayed you and your friends to the military."

She looked for reasons to blame herself, but he wouldn't let her. Couldn't because he well knew what it was like to not have control of your body…or mind. "None of it was your fault."

"Then whose is it? I'm the one who did these things. All the general had to do was say a few letters and numbers before he was able to use me to escape. I can't be trusted."

"We can fix that."

"But how do you fix the fact I killed someone?" she cried. "I killed that smug bastard with my bare hands, and I liked it, Joe. Laughed while he begged. Smiled as he screamed."

"We all do things we're not proud of. But in this case, given what he did to you, and probably planned to do again, I'd say you were more than justified."

She struggled to push free, and he set her down on her feet. She stepped from the shower, dripping water onto the floor as she hugged herself. "You should have left me in the pod."

"I wasn't about to let you die."

"Even if it's what I wanted? You heard the general. I'm a whore. And a failure, even as a cyborg," she spat bitterly. "How could you want me? I don't even want myself." She burst into tears and sank to the floor, her whole frame shivering.

He crouched at her side, trying to swallow his rage when she flinched at his touch.

"What do you remember?" he asked softly, pulling her into his arms. She went stiffly at first then melted, flinging her arms around his neck to sob softly.

"He did something to make me remember. And now I can't forget all the horrible things. They used me, Joe, just like he said. Passed me around like some sexbot with no feelings."

"It wasn't your fault."

"I know that, but do you know what's worse?" she sobbed against his chest. "They ordered me to like it. Made me beg for more when they hurt me. Made me cry out in pleasure even as I wanted to sob."

An icy rage filled his veins while vengeance boiled beneath his skin. "When we get to our home world, I will have Einstein find a way to download your memories to me, and I will hunt each and every one of those men down and kill them."

She stilled in his arms and peered at him with tear-stained cheeks. "Why?"

He shouted his words, overcome with anger. "What do you mean why? They hurt you. So now they must die!"

"You would go back to earth and risk capture just to give me vengeance?" She pulled back from him and stared at him, her eyes moist pools of pain. "Are you insane? I'm not worth your life."

"To me you are. I would do anything for you. Anything to take away your pain," he whispered, reaching out to stroke his thumb over her cheek. "I would kill them all. Every single last one. I would make them scream in agony a thousand times for each time they hurt you. Tell me you want them destroyed and I will build the largest bomb the universe has known and send all humans into oblivion. I would take all your pain if I could, little one, take it that you do not suffer."

"You don't know what you're saying."

He grabbed her hand and placed it over his heart. "Since my rebirth as a cyborg, I don't feel much, not even pain. But knowing what was done to you, it tears at me. It hurts, Chloe. It hurts so much."

*

Chloe could only raise her hand and touch in wonderment at the tears that wet his lashes. "You're crying for me?"

He caught her hand and kissed the palm. "I love you, little one. I might not understand how to romance you, or convince you of this truth, but I feel it. It is the most uncomfortable sensation and, at the same time, the most glorious."

"Even knowing I'm far from pure?"

"We've both had things done to our body. Seen our lives stolen from us. But we've broken free from the slavery the humans would have imposed. Fought back to regain our freedom. Do not let the past drag you down. Do not let them win."

"But what about my programming? Solus was right, you know. I am a walking time bomb. Just because I managed to snap out of it and kill the general doesn't mean I won't betray you again."

"Then I shall watch you, we all will for the rest of this voyage until we reach home. We have people who can fix what is wrong with you, Chloe. Make it so that you never have to fear someone imposing their will on your own. Will you trust me on this?"

How could she not when every word he spoke resounded with sincerity? When the look in his eyes said he would do anything for her? When the love in his hug and his tone surrounded her and made her feel safe, like she mattered?

She leaned forward and kissed him, a soft thank you that tasted of salty tears. "You don't have to kill anyone one for me," she murmured.

"But I don't mind. It would be my pleasure."

A watery chuckle escaped her. "I'm sure it would. There is only one thing I truly need though to feel better."

"Tell what it is and I will give it to you."

"Love me, Joe. Love me and promise to never let me go."

"Too easy. I already vowed that."

She gave him a tremulous smile. "In that case then, perhaps you should show me. I think I need some convincing." And a part of her did, some reassurance that what she'd learned hadn't changed how he felt about her. She needed the warmth of his touch to prove to herself what they did hadn't irreparably damaged her. She needed to feel *alive*. And loved.

As if understanding all the things going through her mind, Joe gave her what she craved. He made love to her. His hands roamed her body, stripping her of her sodden clothing, branding her skin as his own with his electric touch. He overwrote the ugly memories with beautiful ones, claiming her skin as his, reminded her that a man's touch could be beautiful.

His eyes regarded her with a smoky reverence that caught her gaze and stole her breath. He leaned in to kiss her, a tender embrace that made her eyes tear up. But she'd had enough of crying. She wanted passion. She flung her arms around his neck and held him close, letting her tongue plunder his mouth with a violent eroticism that soon had them both panting.

They still sat on the bathroom floor, not that she cared. He held her cradled on his lap, his throbbing cock rubbing against her backside. She didn't want to take the time to move. Didn't want to break the spell. Needed him now.

She lifted her bottom until she could feel the tip of his erection probing at her pussy lips. His hands spanned her waist, aiding her in holding her position, and a good thing too because he'd caught one of her nipples in his mouth. He sucked at it and bit at the nub, sending a jolt of pleasure through her.

Her hands threaded themselves in his hair and held him tight to her as she moaned in response to his caresses. Then she keened loudly as she lowered herself on his thickness, stretching around him and taking him fully into her sex, where he belonged.

She bent her head so that their foreheads touched and their breath mingled. She was content not to move for the moment, just savoring the pulsating feel of him inside her, sensing the pounding of his pulse. Alive, that's what those things meant to her, alive and in love and wanted.

"I love you," she whispered.

"As I love you, little one. I will be at your side for eternity, loving you and doing my best to make you happy."

She knew he would. And she would do the same in return, starting now. She rotated her hips, driving him deeper, shuddering at the low rumble that went through him. Again, she shifted, gasping when he dug his fingers into her fleshy cheeks and arched his own pelvis to grind himself against her, probing at her g-spot.

Again and again, slowly, with languorous tenderness, they moved in rhythm, each stroke, each breath, each convulsive tightening bringing them closer and closer to the edge. With an exhalation of his name, she shattered in his arms, squeezing his rigid cock until she felt an answering molten spurt inside her as he found his own pleasure.

Even when the shaking subsided, they didn't move apart, meshed together as one in an embrace she wished could last for a lifetime, but of course didn't.

"Hey, Joe, you're not answering our wireless messages and…Oh, hello there, Chloe. Nice ass." Seth whistled at the end of his compliment.

Cheeks flaming, she buried her face in Joe's shoulder then bit back a laugh as he cursed the cyborg out for not knocking. Then threatened to remove his eyes for looking upon her. Then…

As the threats grew in size and ridiculousness, she smiled. The pain in her psyche wasn't completely healed. The things she'd suffered at the hands of the human military, while surreal as if they'd happened to someone else, would haunt her for a long while, perhaps always. However, with Joe's love and support, she would make it. She would move past all her previous life's human baggage, embrace her cyborg heritage and emerge stronger and happier than before.

And most of all, I'll love. Even better, I'll be loved in return…forever.

Epilogue

Joe paced the waiting area, annoyed that Einstein kicked him out of the operating chamber when Chloe needed him most. Actually, when he needed her most. It killed him to know she underwent delicate surgery and reprogramming without him by her side.

From the moment they landed and she beheld the lush beauty of the planet, she'd been possessed of a single unchangeable mind — to have the human programming that made her a puppet removed. He tried to assure her she didn't need it, that he would take care of her, but she insisted. Her exact words had been, "I don't ever want those bastards to mess with my mind or actions again."

When he railed about the danger, she seduced him until he would have given her anything she wanted. In the end, he agreed because one of the very laws he drafted said cyborgs owned the right to make their own decisions, unless they were defective. If thought incapable, then someone qualified could make important decisions for them. Solus, that traitor, wouldn't help him in this matter, declaring Chloe mentally fit.

So a date was set for her programming. However, because she lacked a wireless transmitter, accessing her BCI for modification required an actual operation where part of her skull was removed. As if that weren't nerve wracking enough for a previously fearless cyborg, fragile brain tissue needed delicate navigation to allow them access to her neural implant. Due to her still mostly human nature, the odds of a mishap occurring were unreasonably high.

What if something happened? What if Einstein's knife and soldering iron slipped at a crucial moment and caused irreparable damage? What if she died? What if...

The dread saw him wearing a groove in the floor as fear and nervousness kept him company. But at least, he didn't pace alone. Solus and Seth kept him company, the former wearing an appropriate glower, while the latter forewent his usual jovial gibberish. A shame because Joe would have liked a reason to hit something.

When Einstein finally emerged, Joe couldn't stop himself from grabbing the other cyborg and slamming him up against the wall.

"How is she? If you killed her, I'll—"

"Relax. The female is fine. We managed to reconnect the neural pathways the military snipped when they messed with her mind. They did some strange things in there that don't make any sense, but I didn't figure you'd want me messing any more than I had to, so I left it alone and took pictures instead. I did however implant and connect a wireless transmitter that we can use in the future in case she requires upgrading or diagnostics. It is functional, as I used it to download the new software that wiped all existing codes from her processor, leaving her one hundred percent in charge of her own mind."

"Thank you," Joe whispered, dropping his friend and brushing his lapels.

"I wish I could have done more. I can't quite give her the same upgrades we have, but I did manage to correct her programming to the extent that her nanos will increase in number and perform at a higher level than they do currently."

"As long as she's okay, that is the only thing of import."

"Your female is fine and already awake. She is asking to see you. Although why she would choose to remain with an illogical, and an admittedly unintelligent, specimen as yourself is still a mystery."

"It's my charm," Joe riposted as he pushed past his friend to go into the room.

Propped up on pillows, looking tired but alert, Chloe threw him a wan smile. "Joe." She held out her arms, and he hurried to her side, carefully scooping her against him, mindful that the incision in her scalp still required time to heal.

"Oh Joe," she whispered, her voice tight with emotion. "It's horrible."

"What is, little one? Are you in pain? Do you want me to kill Einstein? I can if you want," he offered, not entirely joking.

"No, this has nothing to do with me. I'm fine actually."

"Then why do you cry if not from discomfort?"

"I can handle the pain. Einstein gave me some medication to control it. But, my pain pales in comparison to this."

What could be worse than her discomfort? "Tell me what ails you and I will destroy it," he promised.

"There's nothing to kill." She leaned back and clutched at his hands, her eyes gazing at him with a frantic light that frightened him. "Joe, he lied."

"Who lied?"

"The general. He lied, Joe. I'm not the only one."

Joe digested her startling claim as a gasp came from the doorway. Solus entered, followed by Einstein and Seth. "What are you saying?" his friend asked while Joe stroked the back of her hand with his thumb.

"I'm not the only female cyborg out there. I don't know what Einstein did, but I remember things from my testing days, memories I didn't even know were missing. There were thirteen of us in total in the program. Thirteen cyborg women. One died during testing, but eleven women survived with no idea of who they are. Suffering the same abuses I did. We have to help them."

"Then free them I shall," Joe promised, anything to wipe the tears he hated to see.

"I'll come with you."

Before Joe could tell her in no uncertain terms she wouldn't, Solus stepped forward. "No, you need to stay here with Joe where it's safe."

"Besides, this is a job for single cyborgs," Seth interjected. A grin burst free. "Time to let another male have a chance at saving a cyborg damsel in distress. Don't you worry your pretty little shaved head, we'll get your sisters back, Chloe. Every single one. And we won't stop searching until they're all safe." Seth finished his claim with a serious mien, an expression not often seen on his roguish face.

"We'll find them," Solus added, his face and tone equally sober. "And bring them home."

The End, of this story.
Cyborgs: More Than Machines - C791, F814, B785, Aramus and Seth.
More info at EveLanglais.com

Made in the USA
Middletown, DE
10 June 2015